I0452474

"Ted's pastor's heart has melded with his creative mind to bring to life a first-century teenage seeker of God to engage young people desirous to meet Jesus today."

— Pastor Sheilah Fletch, Author of *Forgiven* and *Reconciled*

"I like how Ted leads us into Arava's life and gives background. He weaves into the story various Jewish customs and ideas, which I think is great. To me, that is the one big win of the book: It's a new way to look at a familiar story—through the eyes of a partial outsider but who is Jewish, so she carries with her certain ideas and expectations around the Messiah. That's all compelling, as is what life would have been like working in the high priest's house."

—Rev. Matthew Ruttan, Blogger,
Author of devotional book *Up*

Arava's
Awakening

Arava's
Awakening

Ted Creen

ARAVA'S AWAKENING
Copyright © 2025 by Ted Creen

All rights reserved. Neither this publication nor any part of this publication may be reproduced or transmitted in any form or by any means, electronic or mechanical, including photocopying, recording or any information storage and retrieval system, without permission in writing from the author.

This is a work of fiction. Any references to historical events, real people, or real places are used fictitiously. Other names, characters, places and events are products of the author's imagination, and any resemblance to actual events, places or persons, living or dead, is entirely coincidental.

ISBN: 978-1-4866-2641-0
eBook ISBN: 978-1-4866-2642-7

Word Alive Press
119 De Baets Street Winnipeg, MB R2J 3R9
www.wordalivepress.ca

WORD ALIVE
—P R E S S—

Cataloguing in Publication information can be obtained from Library and Archives Canada.

This book is dedicated to the two grandchildren God has given to my wife, Lorraine, and me: Grace and Jonah. They will discover that their names are included in this story.

Contents

Preface

You are about to meet Arava, a seventeen-year-old servant living in Jerusalem at the time of Jesus. Her life and adventures unfold during a dramatic era, as you will see from following her journey. To deepen your experience, this book frequently uses character names that are closer to the original Hebrew of that age than to our usual English translations. Below is a list of those names beside the English names we see in most Bible translations. The Hebrew name is italicized. Names are listed in the order they appear and are provided as a reference for you as you read through the story. The central character of this book, Arava, has a uniquely Jewish name. You will discover the meaning behind her name as you read.

Benjamin: *Binyamin*
Rebecca: *Rivkah*
Jonah: *Yonah*
Esther: *Hadassah*
Jesus: *Yeshua*
Messiah: *Mashiach*
Deborah: *Dvorah*

Judas: *Yehuda*
James: *Yaakov*
Thomas: *Tau'ma*
John: *Yochanan*
Simon: *Shimon*
Mary: *Miryam*
Ruth: *Reut*
Joseph: *Yosef*
Andrew: a Greek name, which will remain Andrew
John Mark: a Greek name, which will remain John Mark
Characters unique to this story will be given Hebrew names.
The following Jewish festivals are included in this story:
Passover: *Pesach*
Pentecost: *Shavuot*
Sabbath: *Shabbat*
Other Jewish festivals mentioned in this book use their Hebrew names: *Purim* and *Sukkot.*

1

A Close Call

"That was too close!" thought Arava as she quickly ducked to hide behind a massive stone archway. The bright sunshine of a beautiful Jerusalem day had dazzled her, and on her way to the market, she'd been distracted by a group of children in a narrow alley. She enjoyed watching children at play, although doing so made her own carefree childhood seem a long time in the past.

Unfortunately, that had almost caused her to stumble headlong into a group of Roman soldiers. With her heart was thumping inside her chest, she tried to calm herself. An encounter with Roman soldiers might raise some troubling questions. They would want to know who she was and where she was going. As she was out on her own, she certainly didn't want to run into any unpleasant situations.

Arava was a Jewish girl who had grown up under the Roman occupation of Israel. Encountering Roman soldiers and other officials was a regular occurrence. Throughout the country, the occupation was deeply resented. Arava remembered how upset her father had been about the taxes their people were required to pay to Rome. Added to that was the fact that the local tax collectors were Jewish men, recruited by Rome, who often gouged the people for their own benefit. Arava knew all too well how difficult life had been for her family, even though her father had worked a trade as a stonemason. That work had brought in some money, but taxes took too big a portion of it. Despite this, her early life had been happy and secure in Cana of Galilee.

With a glance from behind the archway, Arava breathed a sigh of relief to see that the coast was clear. But she sensed something else nagging at her. As her mind cleared, she realized that those soldiers probably wouldn't have cared about a servant girl like her, anyway. Had they even noticed her? As she looked out into the street, she could see them marching off and hear their boots echoing on the cobblestones. They did make an impressive sight with their polished breastplates and gleaming helmets, complete with swords strapped to their sides. Arava didn't completely understand her fear of all things Roman—it was deep and troubling. She decided to think more about that later.

For now, she had duties to pursue. Only seventeen years of age, Arava worked as a servant in the home of Caiaphas, the current high priest in Israel. She was part of a sizeable group of servants and slaves who worked in the lavish and extensive house provided for Jerusalem's high priest. Her father, Binyamin, had died suddenly four years ago, and the loss of his income had left her mother unable to provide for their household. Arava had two younger siblings, but she was the oldest and had chosen to search out her own future.

And so, she had left her home in Cana to seek a new life in Jerusalem. Arava was fortunate to have secured the position of a servant. It meant she would not be left to beg in the streets. She was all too aware of those who had to survive that way along the streets of the city. Many were crippled, blind, and infirm, and Arava felt a deep sadness for their situation. At times, when she had a few extra dates or figs, she shared with one of those who were lying there.

Arava was tall and strong for her age, intelligent, and curious. The first few months at the high priest's home had been challenging. She'd adapted quickly, however, and with some help from the older servants, had learned what was expected of her. Her fellow servants admired Arava's tenacious zest for life despite the hardships she'd endured.

Arava was often given the task of seeking out and purchasing fresh provisions for Caiaphas's table. She enjoyed this, for it took her through the pathways of the city on her way to the market. Jerusalem was so different from the small town where she'd been raised. It held a maze of narrow streets and twisting alleyways. Each pathway presented a new experience for Arava. She gazed upwards at the stone archways, wondering how they had been built. The pungent smells of cooking intrigued her and made her hungry. Songs of children echoed in her mind long after she had hurried on.

A tremendous mix of people thronged those streets, often speaking a variety of languages different from the Aramaic she spoke. Arava was grateful she had the opportunity to experience so much of the vibrant life happening all around her in this amazing city. Unfortunately, it had also led to her close call with those soldiers today.

Her anticipation heightened as she approached the market's entrance. She recalled her initial shock at the sights and sounds of this place. Growing up in a small town had not prepared her for the intensity of Jerusalem. However, she'd come to savour the sound of the sellers calling out their wares, the scent of exotic herbs and spices, and the sight of what appeared to be total chaos. As her eyes took in the commotion all around her, she was keenly aware of the constant chatter. Other servants, like her, were surveying the stalls, each looking for the best and freshest of provisions. Some were already bartering with the merchants, trying to get larger portions for less of a cost. Arava thoroughly loved her interactions with the market vendors. There were many with whom she had developed close relationships.

One of her favourites was a couple, Mordechi and Rivkah, who had some of the freshest produce in the market. Mordechi was short and stocky. He had a dark, sun-weathered face that always seemed to be wreathed in a warm, welcoming smile. The first time Arava approached his stall, she'd noticed that he had limited use of his left arm. It took her a while to ask about it, but he'd been only too willing to share the story of his life. He had been raised on his family's vineyard plantation. From his earliest days, he'd worked hard caring for the grape vines. Sadly, just after his marriage to Rivkah, an accident had left him with permanent damage to his left arm. Knowing he would not be able to continue in the vineyard, he and Rivkah had sought out a new life in Jerusalem. They'd become very successful shopkeepers, and Arava valued their expertise in all things to do with fruit or vegetables.

As she approached their stall, she called out with her usual, "Shalom, Mordechi! Shalom, Rivkah!" Mordechi was standing behind a table laden with produce and responded in kind. "Shalom to you, too, Arava. What can I get you today? What does Caiaphas want for his dinner table tonight?" Arava took some time to look over all that was laid out on the tables. "Those figs—they must have just arrived. They look so fresh!" she exclaimed. "Ah, you have such a good eye, Arava. Yes, they just came in from Jericho."

Arava remembered that tomorrow evening was the beginning of Shabbat. That meant even more preparations for the coming day. God had commanded his people to observe one day of rest each week. It was one of Arava's favourite times. After preparing and serving supper to the high priest and his family and entourage, the servants would withdraw to their own quarters and share the simple ritual to welcome Shabbat. On the evening of Shabbat, it began with the lighting of candles, together with blessings and eating a special bread. Often, she would be chosen to light those candles. This brought back warm memories of her childhood, when her mother lit them and her family recited the blessings together.

Rivkah appeared from out back. Her flaming red hair and high energy always seemed to burst on the scene. She usually spoke loud and quickly, and Arava, being of a quieter nature, at first found Rivkah to be intimidating. Over time, though, she had come to love this woman with the fiery, blunt nature. Through Rivkah, Arava had gained the confidence to bargain and barter, which was totally acceptable and even expected in the marketplace.

Before Arava could say anything, Rivkah spoke excitedly. "Arava, how good to see you today. I hope Mordechi has been treating you fairly. But just look at you! So tall, with such lovely dark eyes and long hair—but so thin, so very thin! How are you to ever attract a husband? They must be working you too hard up there at the high priest's. Mordechi, make sure Arava gets some of those tasty dates just for herself." She finally took a breath and, turning back to Arava, finished with, "Arava, you take special care of yourself. It will be a busy time with Pesach coming, and who knows what dangers lurk in those alleyways you love to explore? Now, don't forget to get a bag full of dates!"

At that point, Mordechi stepped in again. "I have some pomegranates here, too. I'm sure they would add flavour to the evening meal." Reaching over, Arava carefully felt the pomegranates. Yes, they were excellent, and so she added a good number of them to her basket, along with a generous number of dates. "I added some extra for you. Don't worry, there's no extra cost. Just make sure you have some to share with the rest of the servants tonight." Mordechi smiled. "And blessing to you for Shabbat."

"Blessings to you, too, Mordechi, and shalom to you, Rivkah. And many thanks." With a quick stop at the stall of an olive seller, Arava completed her tasks. Picking up her now-heavier basket, she turned to walk up the hill that led to Caiaphas's home. Arava had to chuckle over Rivkah's outburst. The fact was, no matter what she looked like, Arava was in no position to get married. She thought back to Cana. Most of her childhood friends would be married by now. Many of their marriages had been arranged between the families since the time they were born. Some of them probably even had children by now. Arava shook her head. She was a servant and would continue to be one for the time being. Maybe someday she would have a family of her own.

Arava enjoyed this part of her day. In the afternoon sun, the buildings with their whitewashed exteriors basked in a golden glow. In particular, the temple shone out in all its glory. It was an impressive structure, towering over the rest of the city. Some days she had time to visit the Temple Mount and go up to the plazas surrounding the temple itself. There she could watch the throngs of people going in and out. On special holy days, the shofar would sound from the pinnacle of the temple, and that always sent shivers up her back. One of the most special of holy days was approaching next week. It was called Pesach, and Jerusalem would be full of excitement. She would be busy, as Pesach was an important time for the household of the high priest, and there would be much activity there.

2

Shabbat

Having secured her purchases at the market—thankfully with some time to spare—Arava slowly made her way back home. It gave her time to go over the multitude of thoughts that so often rumbled around inside her mind. She reflected upon the vast changes in her life since coming to Jerusalem. Living and serving in Caiphas's house had initially been quite a shock. As a servant, she'd had ample opportunity to experience the grandeur of the house. It had taken her breath away. The whole complex was huge, including the quarters where the servants lived. Everything about it was lavish.

One thing that constantly amazed Arava was the sheer opulence of the areas where Caiphas and his family lived. The rooms where he met with the religious leaders of the country were almost as impressive. Furniture and decorations had obviously come from faraway places. Arava had seen caravans, laden with goods, wending their way through Jerusalem. Many of those traders from eastern lands brought silks and weavings to the high priest's home.

Despite all the grandeur and beauty, the place Arava enjoyed most was the outside courtyard. It was large and surrounded by a high wall. Entrance to the property was through a guarded gate. The reason she loved the courtyard was that she had found a special place there amongst some ancient olive trees. With their twisting trunks, they seemed to be almost magical. Between those trees was a quiet spot where Arava would go when she was not working—a place to think and dream. The trees provided shade and shelter, which Arava was thankful for on the hot days of summer. It was well away from the busy pathway to the house, where the constant stream of visitors walked to meet with the high priest.

These thoughts took Arava back to the home in which she'd grown up. It was a small two-room building made of bricks and covered in plaster. Yes, it was small, but so were all the other homes in Cana. Floors there were made of dirt, nothing like the beautiful mosaic tile floors she now walked upon. As she was serving the high priest, his family, and guests, Arava's eyes took in the incredible silk wall hangings. The colours and patterns were stunning. When she'd arrived on the first day, she'd had no idea there could be this kind of finery and beauty in the world. It was so different from what she had experienced in Cana. Arava felt she was living in a totally different world now.

She quickly made her way inside and saw the other servants busy preparing the evening meal. One of them was Leah, just a few years older than Arava. The two had become friends. "Well, you certainly took your time getting back from the market," Leah began. "I do hope you were successful!"

"Oh, yes," replied Arava. "The shopkeepers today were so helpful." A second servant approached, a girl named Tirza. Arava was never quite sure what might come out of her mouth.

Tirza spoke rapidly. "It's about time you showed up, Arava. The priests have been so demanding—all afternoon they've been after us to get this place spotless for Passover."

"Just so old Caiaphas can impress his fancy friends," added Leah with a chuckle. "They feast and celebrate, but we do all the work!"

Laying out the provisions she'd acquired at the market, Arava whispered to her friends, "Quiet! We may be overheard, and Caiaphas does not take complaining lightly. Here, just step behind this pillar. I was able to secure a few extra figs for us." After quickly devouring their treat, the three returned to their tasks. The next few hours would be demanding for them all.

The evening meal was served and servants set to the necessary clearing up. The busy time had passed quickly, and Arava sought out the refuge of the courtyard to rest and reflect. Thoughts of home had reignited memories of her father. Life for Arava had been difficult since his sudden death, and for some time, she had tried to put the memories out of her mind. Now she was beginning to remember just how close they had been. Deep pangs of loss accompanied those thoughts. He had been a strong man and had worked hard as a stonemason. Near Cana was a city called Sephora. She remembered her father saying it had been destroyed by Rome after an attempted insurrection. However, King Herod had decided to rebuild it and make the new city an important centre. That meant steady work for people like her father. Her early life together with her younger brother, Yonah, and sister, Hannah, had been peaceful.

Jerusalem had its intrigue, and she loved to explore and experience so many new things. But home was much simpler. Her family had a small plot of land where they were able to grow some vegetables for their meals. They also had a few chickens and two goats, whom Arava had been given the happy task of feeding each day.

Outside the town were hills and vast open spaces. Arava's father had come from Tagba, right on the shore of the lake called Galilee. Her family had often visited there with relatives. She'd loved to explore along the shore, watching the fishermen and their nets out on the water. Fish was a staple item on her relatives' table. Arava had developed a taste for the tender tilapia fish the boats brought to shore. Apart from the sudden storms that occasionally struck from the surrounding hills, Tagba was very peaceful. Arava savoured her memories, grieving how her father's death had changed everything for the family.

That thought brought her back to her current reality. For now, Arava's home was in Jerusalem, and she was thankful she had a place to live and work. At the home of Caiaphas, Arava also had the opportunity to watch the powerful, religious people of her land as they came for important meetings with the high priest. She wondered what Pesach would bring this year. Throughout the city, pilgrims would gather from many parts of the country and even from foreign lands. Arava loved to hear the different languages and listened for any news she could glean from their conversations as she made her way through the market stalls. It was sure to be exciting.

As Arava mulled over her cluttered thoughts, she suddenly recalled the earlier incident with the Roman soldiers. She pondered it again. That episode had awakened deep feelings of anxiety and fear. She asked herself why she had reacted so strongly. What was it that had frightened her so much at the thought of encountering those soldiers? She was determined to seek out the answer.

The following day was busy with preparations for Shabbat. Arava hurried to and from the market with little time to even think. Although she saw a few Roman soldiers along the way, she did not entertain any thoughts of fear. They seemed to be quite occupied with managing the growing number of pilgrims arriving in Jerusalem for Passover. It did cross her mind that perhaps she'd been foolish to entertain such fear as she'd had the previous day. Yet somehow, that encounter with the Romans had rekindled her memories of family and home. She had more to ponder later, as now she had arrived back at the high priest's house.

Approaching the gate, she was greeted by Ezra, the servant who was often given the task of admitting, or not admitting, those coming to see Caiaphas. She wasn't sure how old he was, but with his trim white beard and the constant twinkle in his eyes, Arava sensed he was someone she could trust deeply.

"Shalom, Arava. Have you been able to find something good from the market today?" he called out as he opened the gate for her.

"Shalom, Ezra! Yes, some lovely pomegranates and lots of fresh figs and dates."

"Well, you have such a knack for finding the best for the household. I do hope you were able to secure some good things for yourself and the other servants as well."

"Oh, yes," replied Arava. "Mordechi and Rivkah were very generous today. They're so good to me!"

As the sun set and evening drew over the city, the servants served the Shabbat meal and cleared up as quickly as they could. For now, with the darkness, Shabbat had begun. That meant it was time for the servants to withdraw to their quarters and share the special candles they lit each week.

They gathered in the quiet darkness. Arava was invited to light the two candles from the small oil lamp that would be kept burning through the night. As the candles were lit., Hadassah, one of the more senior servants, waved her hands around the flames three times, gathering the light to her eyes as the blessing was recited:

Blessed are You, Adonai, our God, Ruler of the universe,

Who sanctified us with the commandment of lighting Shabbat candles.

Hadassah reminded everyone of the significance of those two candles: first, to remember, and then, to keep Shabbat. This woman had become somewhat of a mother figure for Arava. She had often gone to Hadassah with her questions and struggles on how to become a worthwhile servant. Particularly, when Arava had first arrived and found everything overwhelming, Hadassah had been patient and understanding and had carefully guided her through the expected duties of a servant in Caiaphas's household. "I do need to say a special thanks to Hadassah," Arava thought in the quiet of the moment.

It had not been easy for Arava when she'd first arrived, but she was grateful to have a place to live and a job to do. Yet, she did sense that being "only a servant girl" was not all that she hoped for from life. At this point, she wasn't sure what that better life might be, or if she could ever achieve it. On this night, it was enough to simply rest in the quiet peace of the candlelight and to remember the early years when it was her own mother who gathered the flame as the family recited the blessing. She treasured the warm memories of those times.

After the candles were lit, the servants shared the braided, sweet-tasting challah bread that had been freshly baked that afternoon. Then Arava quietly made her way to her bed mat, sleepily wondering what the next week would bring.

3

What Arava Overheard

Mornings always came too quickly for Arava. The first few glimmers of daylight peaked through the small window of her room. She shared the room with three other female servants, and she noticed they were already awake. Rubbing her eyes, she knew she must quickly wash, put on a fresh tunic, and hurry to join the rest of the servants who were preparing the morning meal. Arava was kept very busy at her morning tasks. All the while, she anticipated the possibility of a few quiet moments to herself before her other duty of shopping at the market. Yesterday had awakened a lot of thoughts, memories, and questions.

After serving and clearing the morning meal, Arava made her way into the courtyard and to her special place amongst the ancient olive trees. The morning air was fresh as she took some deep breaths to settle herself. Most days, Arava continued a practice she had begun as a child in Cana—she would scatter breadcrumbs for the little doves that fluttered all around her. The other servants found it amusing, but she craved that connection with her past. All day, she carried a little pouch and gathered crumbs into it as she cleared up the daily meals. Now, as she sat in the peace of this place, she spread her crumbs and heard the gentle cooing sounds as the doves descended.

Arava treasured these times to reflect and think. Today she had a lot on her mind and in her spirit. She pondered a dream she'd had just before waking. Perhaps it had been prompted by her memories of home from the day before, of being in the loving care of her family. Her dream had taken her back to a time with her father, who had loved the Hebrew Scriptures. At the Shabbat services he attended in the local synagogue, large scrolls would be taken down and portions from those Scriptures would be read. When he returned, he would sit down with Arava, Yonah, and Hannah to share with them the rich stories of their faith.

In Arava's dream, her father had recounted to her the story of the festival called Purim. For Purim, the story of Hadassah was retold: the story of how the Jewish people had been saved from destruction.

Arava went over it in her mind, trying to recapture the sound of her father's voice in the dream, trying to remember just how he had told her the story. The Jewish people were in exile, but the king had chosen Hadassah, a Jewish woman, to be his wife and the queen of the country. An advisor to the king named Haman had sought to have all the Jewish people killed. He'd talked the king into issuing an edict that commanded all people to bow down to him. Haman knew the Jewish people would not bow down because they worshipped only the one true God. The punishment for not bowing was death! Haman was determined that all Jewish people be eliminated.

Mordechi, Hadassah's uncle, had gone to her, demanding she plead with the king for the safety of her people. For Arava, the words that stayed in her mind were from Mordechi's challenge to Hadassah: "Perhaps you were born for such a time as this!" Through Hadassah's intervention, the Jewish people were saved. Arava had mulled over those words for years now. She distinctly recalled how her father had used that story with words that remained fixed in her heart: "Arava, your mother and I love you very much, and perhaps you, too, have been born for such a time as this."

For Arava, the present time posed a more pressing question. "Am I always to be a servant girl?" she wondered. "Is that the purpose for my life—is that why I was born?" Her thoughts went deeper in the morning quiet. She recalled how, before his death, her father had spent much time studying the prophecy writings, particularly of the promised deliverer, the Mashiach. This person would come from God with a particular anointing. He would bring peace to the land. He would lift the oppression under which the people were struggling. Her father had a deep faith that those Scripture promises would be fulfilled, hopefully in his own lifetime.

Arava was aware of an ache that had been awakened deep inside her. She had been blessed with a close relationship with her father, and then suddenly, one day, he was gone from her life. With her move to Jerusalem, she realized how much the lost contact with her brother and sister meant as well. The ache was something she'd felt before, but not for a long time, and certainly not as strong as it was right now. Working every day in the home of Caiaphas had kept her from dealing with the darker places in her heart. Tears trickled from her eyes as she felt again the pain of her loss. With a deep sigh, Arava decided to leave these thoughts for now. She could hear the voices of others gathering.

Many servants mulled around the courtyard, some resting, others chatting in small groups. Arava made her way to the gate and her friend Ezra. "How is your day, Arava?" he asked.

"I'm thankful for some time just to rest by myself and think," she replied. "As you know, life can be very busy here."

"It's interesting you would say that," continued Ezra. "With Pesach coming in a week, there will be even more demands on us. Indeed, it seems that this year more and more people have been coming to meet with Caiaphas."

"I've noticed that as well. Those well-dressed members of the Sanhedrin have been arriving in increasing numbers."

Almost immediately, an unmistakeable leader approached the gate. The man was tall and well-dressed and carried himself with an air of authority. Ezra greeted him. "Nicodemus, it is always good to see you!" Arava also recognized this member of the council, for he was the only one who had ever taken time to say hello to her.

"What brings you here on Shabbat?" asked Ezra.

Nicodemus replied, "There appears to be a growing concern over what might take place in Jerusalem this Pesach!"

"And if I may ask," questioned Ezra, "what form might this take?"

"For a while now, we've been following a rabbi from Nazareth in Galilee—he goes by the name of Yeshua. Reports have been given of his healing powers. He spends much time teaching, and the people listen attentively. His words hold power—they confront and challenge us! Crowds in growing numbers are following him. The people are attracted to this man, for they believe he may be the promised Mashiach. Caiaphas is worried, for there have been so many others who have claimed to be the Promised One and have attempted to overthrow the rule of Rome and upset our whole religious system. That's why I was summoned to come here today and confer with Caiaphas."

Arava had been standing in the shadows but had overheard everything Nicodemus said. The mention of the word *Mashiach*

17

alerted her. She'd just been thinking about how her father had often used that word. Suddenly she recalled that he'd sought out a teacher named Eliam who professed to be the Mashiach. She remembered her father's hope that this man would arouse the people to free themselves of bondage to Rome and its crushing taxes. Then, they would take back the land and restore the Jewish faith in God.

Such memories caused Arava to be curious about this new so-called Mashiach Nicodemus was talking about. Why would Caiaphas and the Sanhedrin be so concerned about him? She leaned forward to catch more of the conversation. "We have heard," Nicodemus was saying, "that this Yeshua and his followers have come from Galilee to Jerusalem for Pesach. I have spoken with him, but he certainly did not appear to be a revolutionary. However, with the city so packed with pilgrims, things could easily get out of hand. Caiaphas doesn't want to take any chances. If I can, I will try to go tomorrow to the eastern gate of the city, for it is said this Yeshua is planning to make a grand entrance."

This was intriguing news to Arava—a Mashiach from Galilee. Even though he'd sought after the Mashiach, her father had never mentioned a rabbi named Yeshua living in Nazareth. Why would someone from there be of such concern? She wondered whether she could get away after serving the morning meal and be able to see this Mashiach entering the city. Would there be an uprising, a revolution? Would the people join with Yeshua and overthrow Rome?

Tonight, she promised herself, she would get to sleep as early as possible and be ready for an adventure the next day. With that, she silently made her way inside to prepare for serving the evening meal to Caiaphas and his family. And, from all appearances, to others of the Sanhedrin who would no doubt be coming to discuss this Yeshua from Galilee.

4

On a Donkey?

Arava awoke excited. She had slept well and was ready for today's adventure. She dressed quickly and joined the others to serve the morning meal. Immediately following the clean up, she was free and quickly worked her way through the narrow streets to the southern entrance of the temple.

As she passed the Temple Mount, she gazed up at the massive structure towering over Jerusalem. That view never ceased to amaze Arava. Even the foundation stones were astounding. They were huge! She wondered exactly how the workers had brought them there and put them in place. Sometimes she had climbed the steps to the plazas that surrounded the temple itself, being careful to go only as far as the Court of Women.

Today she paused to take in the vista once more. In the centre of the mount was the temple, dazzling in the morning sun, for it was clad in white marble and gold and had massive bronze entrance doors. From what she'd heard at Caiaphas's house, King Herod had undertaken a massive rebuilding of the temple. It was certainly impressive.

She knew that inside was the Holy of Holies, where the Ark of the Covenant had been placed. Moses' stone tablets with the Ten Commandments lay inside. The very presence of God was believed to dwell in that place. Having been in the service of the high priest, she knew that only he was allowed to enter that sacred domain, and that only once a year—on the Day of Atonement when the sins of the people were cleansed for another year.

She knew that soon, at Pesach, the Temple Mount would be overrun with pilgrims. Sacrifices would be offered to God through the priests. Her father had spoken often of his desire for the family to travel to Jerusalem and celebrate the special feasts at the temple. Once, he had come to celebrate Pesach in Jerusalem with a small group from the Cana synagogue. When he'd returned, he had shared a blessing the pilgrims chanted as they approached the temple. Their family had sung it often, and so, here before the great temple, Arava softly sang it again.

> *Enter his gates with thanksgiving.*
> *Enter his courts with praise.*
> *Give thanks to the Lord and praise him.*
> *For the Lord is good and his love is eternal*
> *And his faithfulness lasts forever.*
> > *The Lord is good, and his love is eternal.*
> > *His faithfulness lasts forever and forever.*

Her father had always wanted to return to Jerusalem and the temple but never made it back. It occurred to Arava that she already had spent three years living in this holy city. *Father*, she thought, *today I am standing at the foot of the Temple Mount. I hope to glimpse the one who might be the Mashiach you sought for yourself. Perhaps the redemption of our people will now take place, as you had hoped.*

Arava quickly made her way to the eastern wall of the Temple Mount and the gate that was set inside it. It was a dramatic place to be, as it overlooked the Kidron Valley across to the Mount of Olives. She had seldom been in this part of the city, and she took a few moments to savour the view. If she was correct, this was the place where Yeshua might be arriving. She strained her eyes to look down into the valley, then up the slope on the other side. *What might this grand entrance be like?* she asked herself.

Her contemplation was suddenly interrupted by a procession making its way up from the valley toward the Temple Mount and eastern gate. It appeared Nicodemus had been correct. Arava carefully made her way toward the gate, hoping to encounter the procession when it arrived. She could hear shouting and singing, but she couldn't make out a clearly identifiable Mashiach figure amidst the noise and chaos.

The procession drew near. Where was Yeshua the Mashiach? People were pulling branches from the palm trees and waving them, shouting, "Hosanna!" and "Hallelujah!" As Arava moved closer, she could make out voices proclaiming words from the Scripture she'd heard before: "Blessed is the one who comes in the name of the Lord!" She was intrigued to hear that many of those voices held the same accent as hers, a Galilean accent. Of course, she remembered, Nicodemus had said that Yeshua came from Nazareth in Galilee.

Arava was confused. The procession had advanced close to where she stood. Still, she could not make out anyone resembling a Mashiach. As the crowd cleared a little, she realized that the person everyone was praising was a man riding on a donkey. *How can this be the one to deliver our people?* she wondered, yet this throng of followers appeared joyful and excited. Now they approached the point of going through the gate into Jerusalem itself. *Where are they going? Is there danger ahead?*

She recalled Nicodemus's concern about the potential danger this proclaimed Mashiach might bring to the city. The high priest and Sanhedrin seemed to be on high alert due to his arrival. To Arava, he didn't appear to be any threat at all. He was riding on a donkey, of all things, not a white stallion! He appeared... well, rather ordinary. He was not wearing anything outstanding that might set him apart. Just what would the true Mashiach look like? It suddenly struck her that she really had no idea. What had attracted her father to Eliam?

She followed the procession as it arrived at the Temple Mount. Yeshua had dismounted and stepped forward to lift his eyes to the magnificent temple that had so impressed Arava. Yet as she made her way closer, she could see tears in his eyes. He spoke words of sorrow: "If only Jerusalem knew the true way of peace."

The people continued to follow Yeshua into the city, still calling out, "Hosanna!" Arava recognized some of the religious leaders who had come to meet with Caiaphas now moving amidst the crowd. She searched their faces and thought she recognized Nicodemus, but with all the people, she wasn't sure it was him. As she watched, a few of the religious officials stepped forward. Arava could sense the deep anger in their voices as they confronted Yeshua. "Rabbi, this could get out of hand. Tell these followers of yours to stop all the shouting and singing!"

Arava turned to hear Yeshua's reply. "I tell you, if these people keep quiet, even the stones here will start shouting!" Well, there certainly were a lot of stones in this place. How odd this all felt! She had to admit feeling somewhat disappointed. Her father had studied the Scriptures for promises about the Mashiach. He had sought out the man Eliam who had professed to be the Anointed One. Overhearing the conversation at the gate between Ezra and Nicodemus had awakened hope in her. Caiaphas was so apprehensive about this Yeshua that Arava felt perhaps it was finally the time for change. However, her hope didn't fit with what she'd just witnessed. A Mashiach on a donkey? With palm branches left scattered on the pathway around her, Arava prepared to retrace her steps back to the home of the high priest.

5

A Surprising Touch

As she turned to leave, Arava was startled by a hand laid upon her shoulder. A voice called out, "Arava, it must be you. I haven't seen you for years, but it must be you. You look so much like your mother!" Arava turned to face the speaker. It took a moment to recognize her Aunt Dvorah. Even though it had been many years, she rejoiced at seeing such a familiar figure from her past. Dvorah obviously felt the same way as the two embraced.

Dvorah was the younger sister of Arava's mother, Sarah. She was taller than Sarah but had the same strong features. The two families had lived close to each other in Cana when Arava was very young. They'd shared so many special times together celebrating births and the festivals of the faith. Arava particularly enjoyed Dvorah's love of life. Her aunt had a curiosity that resonated with her. They'd shared many adventures, exploring the hillsides and valleys surrounding Cana. Arava had been twelve years old when Dvorah had married Jesse and moved to Capernaum to develop a trade together. Their business consisted of dyeing fabrics in multitudes of colours.

At almost the same time, both Arava and Dvorah exclaimed, "What are you doing here?"

Arava went first, filling in her aunt on the events of the past few years. "I've been in Jerusalem for almost three years now," she said. "I came here today because of the concern surrounding Yeshua that's swirling around the high priest's house. I overheard someone talking about this entrance into Jerusalem, and I was curious. So here I am!"

Dvorah surprised her niece by confiding that she'd become Yeshua's follower while he was in Capernaum. "Over this past year, I sat at his feet as he taught and watched as he healed many people. I was very impressed with this rabbi, so I talked with his followers. He had gathered twelve close disciples around him, and I spent time with many of them. I wondered if perhaps he really was the Anointed One, the Mashiach. And so, when Yeshua decided to come to Jerusalem for Pesach, I joined the group of people who would travel with him. Jesse felt confident that for a few weeks he could handle the work in our dye shop."

Arava felt relieved to meet up with someone from her past, someone so important to her. "All this talk of Mashiach has been very confusing for me," confessed Arava. "Today I saw the crowd with their joy and excitement, but the Anointed One riding on a donkey just doesn't make sense. How could someone like that deliver our nation? I know my father sought after someone who claimed to be the Mashiach, but now he is gone. I do wonder about this Yeshua. Do you really believe he is the Mashiach?"

Dvorah took a deep breath. "How much do you know about how your father died?" she finally asked.

Memories suddenly flooded Arava's mind. "When we got the news that he'd died, it caused so much turmoil in our family," she started, "and that ended with everyone trying to move on. We just stopped talking about Father. It was too painful for us."

"Arava, do you think about your father now?"

She felt safe to share her feelings. "Yes, especially in these last few days—so many thoughts have returned. I had pushed away my memories because it hurt to realize that Father was gone. Lately, though, some warm thoughts about my life with him have returned. I've had so many glimpses of how much he meant to me, how much he taught and guided me when I was growing up. But then I also have dark, painful thoughts about how much his death has changed my life, and how much our family has suffered. Deep down inside, I miss him now more than ever. I feel like his death has left a deep, dark hole in my heart."

"We need to find a quiet place to talk," replied Dvorah. The two of them made their way down the slope from the temple to a small grove of olive trees. They sat down, and Dvorah slowly explained what she knew about Arava's father and his involvement in the group of Eliam's followers. She reflected upon how much Benyamin had loved the synagogue and the Torah and all the teachings.

"Oh, yes," replied Arava, "some of my best times were with Father and my brother and sister as he retold the stories of our faith."

Dvorah explained how Benyamin had studied the prophetic passages about a coming Anointed One who would redeem the Jewish people—indeed the whole world. "Your father had so much hope in those promises. He firmly believed they would finally come true." Arava interrupted with a heartfelt question about what had happened to her father and Eliam.

"One day," began Dvorah, "the call went out that it was time for the full manifestation of the Mashiach. They would begin a march in Galilee, a march that would gather the entire nation by the time they reached Jerusalem. Just outside of Tiberias, they were confronted by a brigade of Roman soldiers. Someone in Eliam's group drew a sword and attacked a soldier. The Romans responded with brute force, killing that man and Eliam." Dvorah took another deep breath and continued. "Sadly, Arava, your father was caught up in the chaos, and he, too, was killed that day."

Arava felt her heart would stop beating. Tears rose in her eyes. She finally understood the fear that had been lurking deep inside of her. Fierce emotions welled up, and she was surprised by a surge of anger. *Why, Father? Why did you allow yourself to be deluded by that false Mashiach? Why did you take the risk of following him? How could you have left us abandoned and vulnerable?* Arava was shocked at the intensity of the feelings that had suddenly surfaced. But just as suddenly, she felt guilty for harbouring them. She still held a deep love for her father. She said a silent prayer for understanding to help clear her mind of these conflicting thoughts.

Arava now realized where her fear of the Roman soldiers arose from. She carried both anger at Rome and a fear of its soldiers. But she also felt a strange relief at finally confronting the painful reality she'd been carrying for so long. She choked back deep sorrow at the thought of her father following his heart to the death. What would he think of Dvorah seeking out Yeshua, or of her own growing curiosity about him? After a time of silence, Arava spoke up. "What do you see in this Yeshua, that you would follow him to Jerusalem?" she asked her aunt.

"It's difficult to fully explain. When I listen to Yeshua teach, I sense that, for once, I am hearing the truth from God, not just messages from Pharisees or other teachers. His message is one of love and peace, and when I am in his presence, even in a large crowd, I feel the flowing of a healing, forgiving love. Yeshua does not speak of revolt—rather, his message is about building God's Kingdom of peace. We are all to help make it happen."

Dvorah paused and closed her eyes in reflection. "When he speaks, it's as if he's looking right at me and assuring me that God loves and cares for me. It is the same for everyone who has followed him. There is such love that I cannot understand the opposition by the religious authorities. It doesn't seem right to me. We all sense the danger growing around us even as we witness the love of Yeshua in healing and comforting the wounded and poor. I have come to Jerusalem to share Pesach together with him and his followers. No matter what happens, I will continue to follow him. I truly believe that Yeshua is from God himself. I hope that helps you, Arava."

It did help somewhat, but Arava's mind and spirit were still in turmoil, what with everything that had taken place that day. Thanking Dvorah, she hoped they could soon meet again during the week. "I know it will be a hectic week, what with Pesach and so many religious leaders coming to the home of the high priest. But I often have time for myself after serving the morning and evening meals. If you come by then, just tell Ezra at the gate that you know me."

With that, the two women parted, and Arava hurried back to assist with the evening meal. The small flicker of hope that had been awakened within her now joined with the anticipation of another meeting with Dvorah. Something might come of this Yeshua after all. She prayed that the answer would somehow come to her over the next few days of Pesach.

6

Turmoil and Fear

Tension and fear continued to build that whole week leading up to Pesach. Arava could sense it all around her as she went about her duties to Caiaphas. There was a constant parade of religious leaders, and even some Roman officials, all seeking an audience with the high priest. Rumours abounded, whispered through the hallways and discussed late into the night in the courtyard.

She may have been "only a servant girl" of seventeen years, but Arava's natural curiosity led her to listen in on every rumour, and to catch snatches of conversation between the leaders and officials whenever she could. It was fascinating and troubling at the same time. It led to an increased turmoil in her mind and heart. For most of the whispers and conversations revolved around Yeshua. Increasingly, Arava heard talk of what he stood for and why he seemed to be such a threat to Caiaphas and those in his circle.

One morning, Arava sat by the olive trees enjoying the warm sunshine. It was the day before Pesach, and she had much to mull over. She thought back to her visit with Dvorah and everything they had talked about. Even with the hectic week she'd had so far, Arava continued to think deeply about her father. The revelation of how he had died burned deep inside her heart. He had been so convinced that Eliam was indeed the long awaited Mashiach. It continued to trouble her that his quest had ended in death. Now there was this Yeshua from Galilee whom Dvorah had followed to Jerusalem. Dvorah felt that Yeshua was sent by God to spread a message of love and peace. That appealed to Arava, but her mind was still swirling with confusion over it all.

Then there was a conversation she'd overheard in the courtyard the night before. Three of the Sanhedrin had come to meet with Caiaphas. Many of the council had visited over the past few days, but these three had lingered around the warming fire. Arava had silently crept forward, hoping to hear fresh news about Yeshua. The three men appeared to be members of the Sadducee party, judging from their fine clothes and high language. From what she could determine, the talk was indeed about Yeshua.

It appeared he had entered the temple courts and confronted those working at the tables—the tables where people exchanged their money for temple currency to purchase sacrifices. The authorities were truly alarmed, for Yeshua had overturned the tables and scattered the money changers with fierce and holy anger. It amounted to a serious threat to proper temple order. They were eventually joined at the fireside by two members of the Pharisee party who were equally alarmed about the day at the temple.

This did not make sense to Arava. She thought back to the image of the man on a donkey riding through the city gate. She remembered the joyous cries of "Hosanna!" *Why would he go to the temple and do something so violent?* she wondered. As she listened, she became more alarmed. The religious officials shared about their meeting with the high priest, and from what Arava could determine, the talk had turned to what to do about Yeshua. Caiaphas had confided that he wanted this so-called Mashiach to be killed!

Arava shuddered at the thought. Again, her mind reflected on the man on the donkey—so peaceful—and on Dvorah, so full of admiration for him. Now it seemed as if the entire council was alarmed. The final thing Arava heard was one of the men stating, "Well, if Caiaphas gets his way, and I am sure he will, Yeshua will be quickly eliminated. What was it the high priest said? 'Yes, it is better for one man to die than for the whole nation to be in an uproar!'" With that, the group had departed.

Arava made her way over to Ezra at the gate. "Shalom, Ezra. You have been very busy these days with all the people arriving to see Caiaphas."

"Yes, it certainly has been challenging to determine who to allow in and who to send away," he replied. "But it has been troubling too. There's something going on, and I fear things are not good right now—with Pesach just a day away."

Arava paused for a moment and then responded, "I can understand. I, too, have been hearing rumours going around in the halls and in this courtyard the last few days. It all seems to revolve around someone named Yeshua."

Ezra replied, "That certainly is the name I hear mentioned over and over. What I don't understand is why the high priest would be so agitated over this one man."

"Oh, I wanted to ask you, Ezra... did a woman named Dvorah come by and ask about me?"

"I almost forgot!" Ezra exclaimed. "Yes, she did, earlier this morning. But you weren't out here yet. I told her you were probably still serving the morning meal. She said that if you could get to the market tomorrow, she would meet you there midmorning by the entrance. She said she had things to purchase for a Pesach seder." That would work out fine, thought Arava, as she, too, could arrange to get supplies for Caiaphas's seder tomorrow evening.

Arava and Ezra talked for a few more minutes before they were suddenly interrupted by the abrupt appearance of a man at the gate. He was wrapped in a dark tunic, almost hiding his face with it. He appeared to be very agitated. Demanding entrance, he asserted that he had important business with the high priest. Arava couldn't clearly see the man's face, but something about him caught her attention. Why, it was his accent! He must be from Galilee. Perhaps he was one Yeshua's followers, but then why would he want to meet with Caiaphas?

Ezra asked more questions of the man. Who was he, and what was his business? Arava thought she heard the word *Yehuda* and that he had important information for the high priest. Reluctantly, Ezra opened the gate and admitted him. He brushed past Arava without speaking and hurried to the house.

Just what she needed, Arava thought. Even more mystery surrounding Yeshua. But then, thankfully, she'd be meeting with Dvorah tomorrow, and hopefully some of this confusion might be cleared up. All this pulled her back to the thoughts and emotions surrounding her father. Arava desired to know as much as she could about Yeshua. Was he the true Anointed One of God, sent to restore love and peace to the people, the Mashiach her father had so desired? As Arava made her way back to her quarters, a final thought arose in her mind: Could this Yeshua bring love and peace into her own life as he had for Dvorah? Perhaps she would learn more tomorrow.

7

Preparations

After a restless night, Arava awoke and readied herself for what she knew would be a full and busy day. Pesach was celebrated with a special meal, a seder. During that meal, specific foods were eaten, each one symbolizing aspects of the story of Moses and of God's deliverance of the Hebrew people from slavery in Egypt. Every family would celebrate this story with their own Pesach seder. Arava would secure ingredients for the high priest's household seder at the market; plus, she would get some extra food for the servants' own seder.

To prepare for Pesach, every home was required to rid itself of leaven. Part of the exodus story related the Hebrews' hurried departure after Egypt's Pharoah had finally given permission for them to leave. They didn't have time to wait for their dough to rise, so they ate unleavened bread just before they left. At the Pesach seder, only unleavened matzah was eaten. Therefore, it was traditional as a preparation for Pesach to totally cleanse the house and ensure no leaven was left behind. That cleaning had already begun for her fellow servants in the large house, and it needed to be completed before nightfall.

Arava was somewhat thankful she didn't have to help with that cleaning. Her task was to secure special seder supplies at the market today. She planned to purchase bitter herbs for the seder and had also been instructed to find ingredients for charoset: apples, dates, nuts, and pomegranates. The bitter herbs represented the suffering of the Israelite slaves in Egypt. Arava looked forward to the sweet charoset, which stood for the mortar the Hebrew slaves used for their brick building in Pharoah's construction projects.

More importantly for Arava, she planned to meet her Aunt Dvorah at the market. There was so much more to ask her. Mystery and intrigue at the home of the high priest had been building throughout this week. What was going to happen to Yeshua and his followers? Arava hurried to gather with the rest of the servants in preparing the morning meal. Since she had those important errands to pursue, she was allowed to leave the household early and was glad to head to the market.

Making her way down the narrow streets and alleyways she had come to know so well, she soon arrived at the market entrance. Pausing to look around, she didn't see any sign of Dvorah, but she was early. It was not yet midmorning. She made her way to her favourite stall and called out, "Shalom, Mordechi! Shalom, Rivkah! I'm here for the Pesach provisions for the high priest."

"Ah, I thought you would be here this morning," replied Mordechi, "and it is good you have come early, for as you can see, it is already very busy. The city is filling up with pilgrims, and this will be a good day for us merchants. We'll probably run out of supplies before midafternoon." Thankfully, Arava was able to get everything she needed from Mordechi, plus some free extras for the staff to share when they celebrated their own seder.

Wishing a blessed Pesach to Mordechi and Rivkah, she made her way back to the market entrance. Thankfully, Dvorah was there waiting for her. With her were two others Arava assumed to be followers of Yeshua. Dvorah greeted her and introduced her to Yakov and Andrew. They wore the simple clothing of common people and didn't appear particularly special. She could tell they'd come from working backgrounds with their scraggly beards and calloused fingers. Arava felt a bit nervous at meeting these disciples yet was eager to have her questions answered.

"Arava, these are indeed disciples of Yeshua," Dvorah said. "They've travelled with him for over three years and have experienced so much!"

Andrew spoke up. "When Dvorah told us about you and all your questions about Yeshua, I admit I was suspicious. You work in the household of Caiaphas, after all, and we disciples have much to fear from the religious leaders surrounding him."

Yakov added, "The Pharisees have been hounding Yeshua for a long time. Now that we're in Jerusalem, the danger has increased. We felt you might be here to watch us and report back to Caiaphas."

"I assure you," replied Dvorah, "that Arava is a close relative, and you can trust her even if she is Caiaphas's servant. She's very curious about Yeshua, and for good reason. You see, her father followed a false Mashiach named Eliam in Galilee."

Arava spoke up. "I remember how passionate my father was in searching for the true Mashiach. He fervently believed God would send that special one. When I began hearing about Yeshua, it brought back memories of my father's yearnings. I guess I share those now too. That's why I'm so curious about Yeshua."

Yakov nodded. "Yes, we've heard about the prophet Eliam and what took place with him and his followers. I am sorry your father was swept up in that movement and sorry for how it all ended for him. But I do honour him for searching for the Mashiach. We truly believe we've found him in Yeshua." Arava was gratified that these disciples trusted her and that she, in turn, could approach them with the many questions that had been swirling in her mind.

Andrew explained how he and the others had become disciples. "Like you, Arava, we are all from Galilee. That's where we first met Yeshua. Some of us grew up fishing on the lake, near the town of Capernaum." *That would certainly explain the rough hands*, Arava thought to herself.

Yakov added, "On a warm, sunny day three years ago, we were cleaning our nets from the night before when Yeshua suddenly approached on the shore, calling out to us. He challenged us right then and there to follow him. He told us that, from then on, we'd be fishing for people."

"With hardly another thought, we agreed to go with him," said Andrew. "Something about him drew us in a way we'd never experienced before."

Yakov's strong voice broke in. "Being with Yeshua has been amazing. At times it's been hard to believe all the miracles! But we've seen these things with our own eyes. Blind people getting back their sight, crippled ones healed and walking! Arava, you can witness these things for yourself if you join us."

Arava felt a freedom to share her inner turmoil with these disciples; after all, they were friends of Dvorah. "I watched as Yeshua arrived in Jerusalem with everyone singing and praising and waving branches they'd cut from the trees. That's where I met Dvorah again. I had not seen her since I came here from Galilee. She told me about Yeshua, about his teaching and the miracle healings. I wanted to understand just how Yeshua was different from the one my father sought after."

Arava paused to collect her thoughts and then continued. "You see, my father deeply studied the Scriptures. He was very aware of the promise of the Anointed One, the Mashiach. He truly hoped and prayed for peace to come to our land and our people. But he died with his hopes unfulfilled. That tore apart our family, and I was fortunate to find a position here in Jerusalem that gave me shelter, food, and a small amount of money to save."

Then Arava remembered some of the information she'd gleaned during the past few days. "In the hallways and courtyard of Caiaphas's home, I've overheard much talk of Yeshua lately. Religious officials of the Sanhedrin and Sadducees have been coming and going all week. I heard them say that Yeshua had entered the temple courts and caused a great disturbance, overturning the tables of those changing money and selling sacrifices. I cannot see how that would be the same Yeshua I watched on the back of the donkey."

Yakov had been listening carefully. "You must understand why Yeshua was upset at the situation with the moneychangers. To purchase a sacrifice at the temple, say a pair of doves, you must exchange your Jewish or Roman coins for temple currency. That would be fine, except that the moneychangers charge a high fee for the exchange. Basically, they're cheating the people. It's the poorer people like you and me who are the victims, while the moneychangers, like the tax collectors, grow rich. I believe the religious leaders are all a part of that."

Andrew added, "Yeshua really does care about us. That's why the situation in the temple courts made him so angry. It wasn't right. As he said, 'The temple should be a place of prayer, not a den of thieves.' If you could meet him, Arava, you would receive that same love and compassion. That's why I've left everything to follow him."

This helped Arava comprehend more of Yeshua's ministry. It also brought to the surface her deep concern for his followers in Jerusalem. She continued, "I have been hearing some dangerous voices. It seems Yeshua is very threatening to the high priest and the whole Sanhedrin. I overheard a few of them in the courtyard talking about that incident in the temple courts and how angry it made Caiaphas. They went so far as to say that Caiaphas may already have decided to have Yeshua killed. It was something about having one man die rather than cause an uproar in the whole land. I know what it's like around the high priest. I truly believe this is a serious threat to Yeshua and perhaps to you too."

Andrew spoke up. "Yes, we know what you are talking about. We've felt the growing opposition to Yeshua over these past months. And it's only increased since we arrived in Jerusalem. I believe Yeshua realized the risk in coming here, what with the high priest and all the Sanhedrin centred in the city. However, he seemed to have such a desire to celebrate Pesach with us here in Jerusalem this year. Maybe he senses it could be the last time."

Yakov remarked, "I remember how one of us, Tau'ma, declared on the way to Jerusalem that we might as well stay with Yeshua even if it meant dying with him. Andrew's brother, Shimon, the bold and brave one, declared that no matter what, he would stand beside Yeshua. I don't know exactly what will happen. What I do know is that these past three years travelling with Yeshua have changed my life completely. I feel fear all around me, but I know that God will be with us."

With that, Dvorah and the two disciples set out to prepare for their Pesach seder with Yeshua. Arava bid them goodbye and warned them to be careful. Then she, too, realized how much time had passed and hurried back to the home of the high priest. All the talk of the day swirled around Arava's head. She sensed the intrigue coming to a critical stage now that Pesach was about to begin. What might the next hours bring?

8

A Threatening Pesach

In the growing darkness of the evening, the staff prepared and served the evening meal. This meal, however, was different, for it was Pesach and the meal was a special seder meal. For Caiaphas's staff, this meant that as soon as the household seder was finished, they would withdraw to their quarters and share their own seder. Arava had waited for this night with anticipation and a tinge of anxiety. It would bring back more memories of growing up and sharing such seders with her family. Pesach seder meals were meant to be shared in family groups.

This time her memories were of her mother. Arava had been forced to leave the family home in Cana after her father's death. Both Arava and her mother had agreed that she was old enough to seek a life away from home. It would allow her mother and younger siblings to manage on their meager resources. With much anticipation, Arava had made her way to Jerusalem and her new life. It was on nights like this, festival nights to be shared in family homes, that she missed her mother and Yonah and Hannah. Arava whispered a prayer that, as her family back in Cana shared their Pesach seder, they would receive a special blessing and know that she loved them very much.

Arava continued to responsibly fulfill her duties, but the events of the past few days had awakened many jumbled thoughts about her father, her home, and now her mother. It was her mother who lit the Shabbat candles and led the blessings during their family's Pesach seder. Arava realized how much she was missing her mother on this night. She hadn't been able to return to Cana and visit her since coming to Jerusalem. It would have been a journey of a few days—dangerous unless she travelled with others. Arava determined that one day she would return home for a visit.

There was the underlying anxiety of this week in Jerusalem as well. The priest's home had been full of snatches of conversation and constant rumours about Yeshua. Complicating Arava's feelings was her own connection with Yeshua following her meeting with Dvorah. All of this filled her thoughts as she made her way to the servants' quarters with some of the elements for their seder. She wondered about the Pesach those disciples would share with Yeshua. She worried about the danger that faced his little band of followers. There was something growing deep inside of her—it had begun as she watched Yeshua ride into Jerusalem on a donkey.

During her time with Dvorah, an awakening had taken place. Fresh hope was rising in her, for both herself and her people. "May Yeshua be safe this night," Arava prayed. She realized how much more she wanted to discover about him—how much she longed to be near him—to hear his teaching and see the miracles Dvorah had described.

The elements had been carefully laid out on a small, low table. Three pieces of the unleavened matzah sat alongside a bowl that Arava knew was filled with salt water. On a larger plate, lay the simple elements for the seder: a boiled egg, horseradish, parsley, and the sweet charoset that Arava loved. There was also the shank bone from the lamb that had been roasting all afternoon. She remembered with gratitude sharing those same elements with her family during childhood. The seder was ready and all gathered to recite the opening blessing:

> *Blessed are You, Adonai our God, Ruler of the Universe, who has kept us alive, sustained us, and brought us to this season.*

Arava pushed all the conflicting thoughts to the back of her mind and tried to focus on what was happening. The first question posed in the seder was always, *Why is this meal different from all other meals?* Arava wanted to absorb the special meaning once again. Each element was presented to tell the story of freedom for God's people. Unleavened matzah recalled the hurried meal the Israelites ate before leaving Egypt. Parsley was dipped in salt water, which represented the tears of the Hebrew slaves. The years of slavery were remembered by the eating of bitter herbs.

There were other blessings and then a meal of lamb, left over from the high priest's seder. Just as their small seder was about to end with the sharing of a final cup, loud voices and the sound of running feet disturbed the quiet. The servants rushed to the front doors of the house and saw a frantic scene unfolding in the courtyard.

The temple guard was assembling, along with some Roman soldiers. Arava was alarmed to see swords and clubs in their hands. Some older servants bustled around, assisting with the lighting of torches and distributing of lanterns. As she cautiously made her way into the courtyard, Arava spied Yeshua's disciple from the day before. She remembered him being called Yehuda. "What in the world is he doing here with these soldiers and guards?" Arava muttered under her breath.

Another servant overheard her. "I believe this disciple is prepared to lead the soldiers to Yeshua," the servant said. "I think Caiaphas paid him off." Arava wondered how this would all end up. A ripple of pure fear ran up her spine.

Arava was horrified at what was unfolding before her. *There must be some way to stop this travesty!* she cried inwardly. Yet she realized she was powerless against the combined force of the temple guards and heavily armed Roman soldiers. *What will happen to Yeshua and his followers?* she wondered. Then with a shudder, she realized that her Aunt Dvorah might be in grave danger as well. They had spoken earlier about the possible danger, but this was happening too fast and right before her eyes. With a command, the force moved off, heading to the east. All Arava could do now was wait to hear the news. With panic in her heart and tears in her eyes, she found her usual resting place between the olive trees. This could be a very long night.

9

Beside the Fire

The night closed in, and it was cold. Someone lit the charcoal fire in the middle of the courtyard, and many warmed themselves near it. Arava pulled her tunic close around her as she waited. Another large group of officials arrived, and Arava recognized Annas in their midst. He had been the high priest years ago and was Caiaphas's father-in-law. He was still a very powerful man.

She dozed off for a short time but awoke suddenly when the courtyard erupted again. The soldiers had returned, and there in their midst was Yeshua, bound and pushed along by his captors. Arava wanted to reach out and comfort him, but the crowd was simply too large. She watched as they hustled him inside the house. Caiaphas would now have an opportunity to deal with Yeshua face-to-face! Yet as Arava knew all too well, the high priest had some very strong feelings against Yeshua already. Would the rabbi even have a chance to defend himself?

The courtyard became quiet again, with only a few stragglers hanging around. It felt even colder, so Arava made her way to the fire. Others stood close by, doing the same thing. Even in the darkness, she felt she recognized one of them. When he spoke, she detected a Galilean accent like her own. *This must be one of Yeshua's disciples,* she thought. *Perhaps he can tell me what's going on or how I might help.*

Arava turned toward him. "You were one of those with Yeshua, were you not?" Without a moment's pause, the man shouted out, "No, I don't even know that man!" Arava was startled. She sensed great fear and panic in his eyes. Surely, he must be a disciple, yet he had flatly denied it. He turned away into the darkness, and Arava could see someone else speaking to him.

It was one of her fellow servants. He'd seen this man following behind as Yeshua was led into the high priest's court. "I'm sure you were with Yeshua!" he confronted the follower. Again, with a voice that could be heard throughout the courtyard, the man denied knowing Yeshua. By this time, more people had gathered by the fire, wondering what the commotion was all about.

A third servant confronted the disciple. "You must have been with that Yeshua when he was arrested, for you speak with a strong Galilean accent."

This time the follower's reply rang out for all to hear. "I don't know what you're all talking about. I do not know the man they arrested!" In the distant darkness, a rooster crowed. Arava could clearly see a look of terror cross his face. Deep sobs shook from inside this disciple. With one last look back at the courtyard, the man fled through the gate and into the outer darkness of the city.

Time passed, and despite the cold, it was all Arava could do to stay awake. After a short while, a commotion jolted her into full awareness. Some of the temple guards had brought Yeshua out from the house and were marching him to the gate.

She watched as they headed up the street toward the Temple Mount. A few other servants had come out of the house to follow them. Arava approached them and asked, "Do you know what's happening? Where are they taking Yeshua?" One of them shared what he'd overheard during Yeshua's questioning before Annas and Caiaphas.

The high priests had demanded that Yeshua deny being the Mashiach. They had accused him of claiming the ability to destroy the temple and rebuild it. Caiaphas had cried out, "Blasphemy!" and ordered that Yeshua be taken to King Herod and then to Pontius Pilate, the Roman governor. The religious leaders wanted Yeshua killed, but only the authority of Rome could give the edict to crucify.

Arava wept silently at the thought of what might happen to Yeshua now. Where were his followers? She had seen only one, and he'd denied being a disciple and fled. Where were the rest? What had happened when Yeshua was arrested? Then Arava remembered that her aunt must have been there too. Where was Dvorah now? What might have happened to her?

The courtyard was quiet and empty. Dawn would arrive shortly and with it a new day. With a deep weariness, Arava made her way back to the servants' quarters. There would be no answers to her questions this night, so she found her mat and fell into a restless sleep. Who knew what tomorrow might bring?

10

Strange Darkness

One of the other servants shook Arava awake. She'd only been able to sleep for a few hours. No matter. It was time to prepare and serve the morning meal to the household. Caiaphas was not present, nor were many of the other key leaders. The meal was served silently, as no one really felt like speaking. After clearing and cleaning up, Arava collapsed onto a small stool in the corner of the kitchen. Tirza approached. "Arava, you look terrible! What's going on?"

"What's going on? It seems like everything is going on—and going wrong around here lately!"

Leah joined them, agreeing with Arava. "Such turmoil and chaos, all centred around this Yeshua who claims to be the Mashiach. It seems that Caiaphas really fears this man and the following he's developed."

Tirza replied, "It appears that Yeshua is creating a commotion all over Jerusalem. Caiaphas just wants things to calm down."

"But now I hear they've taken Yeshua to be tried by Pilate—that certainly can't be good in any way," cried Arava.

"Pilate and Rome want peace at any cost. If Yeshua is a troublemaker, he'll be swiftly dealt with," answered Tirza. An uneasy silence descended upon the three servants. *Maybe I'll never have the chance to meet Yeshua myself!* thought Arava. A deep, dark fear gripped her heart. She realized that Caiaphas and the others would be pressuring Pilate to convict Yeshua—in the hopes that they could get rid of him once and for all.

This was a thoroughly unpleasant thought, and Arava determined to apply herself even more fully to her tasks. Tonight would be the beginning of Shabbat, and she was usually sent to the market for supplies. Hopefully that would keep her mind off the frightening things going on around her. Perhaps she'd even meet a few of Yeshua's followers and discover some news.

As Arava made her way through the familiar streets and alleyways down to the market, she sensed an oppression in the air. Perhaps it was just her anxiety about what might be happening with Yeshua. Upon entering the market, however, several shopkeepers remarked on the growing darkness as afternoon approached. Some felt a storm was coming. Others said there was a spirit of death in the air.

Mordechi had heard the rumours and bits of information passed on by people who came to his stall. "I fear the worst for anyone who gets in the way of the powers of this land, whether religious or Roman. Now with Pesach and the streets full of pilgrims, the authorities are keyed up. Anything is possible once they decide to act."

Even Rivkah appeared downcast. She warned Arava once again, "Please be careful. Things could really get worse, and you'd be right in the middle of everything up there in the high priest's house!"

Arava made her purchases. It was now midafternoon, but a sudden inky darkness had descended upon the city. Strange, since nightfall was still hours away. Along with the gloom came a distinct chill in the air. It felt as if life had been suspended and the sun had taken to hiding. Arava wrapped her tunic tightly around her, as much to block out the cold as to somehow protect her from the horrible things that might be taking place. Even her footsteps felt heavy and slow. It was as if the darkness were sitting heavy on top of her.

Ezra greeted her at the gate, but a grave manner replaced his usual exuberance. "Shalom, Arava. Have you heard the news?" Arava trembled at the thought of what that might be. Ezra continued, "They crucified Yeshua this afternoon. Members of the Sanhedrin have just returned with the news for Caiaphas. They seem relieved that, whatever danger this man posed, it has finally been dealt with."

Crucifixion? Arava shuddered in disbelief. *Why, it was only last night Yeshua was arrested! How could all of this have happened so fast?* Arava had seen enough of crucifixion over the past three years to know that Yeshua had suffered terribly that day. It was all she could do hold back her tears. She had so hoped to meet Yeshua and learn more about God's love. Fear gripped her, as well, the fear she'd been holding for Yeshua's disciples and followers—specifically her Aunt Dvorah. What would happen now? She felt that if she could hold herself together for a few more minutes, she might be able to gain some more information. With the oppression and darkness, though, neither she nor Ezra could think of anything more to say.

A dark figure walked out of the house. He frantically rushed toward the front gate where they stood. She recognized him instantly—Yehuda! She stepped forward to ask him about what had happened that day, but she didn't get the chance. He hastily brushed past her and disappeared through the open gate.

"That man came back just a short time ago, insisting on seeing the high priest. I was reluctant to admit him again, but I did. His conversation with Caiaphas must not have gone well, judging from how violently he left," Ezra commented. Arava added the mysterious episode to her mental record of the last few days.

Right now, her duties beckoned, and she joined the other servants inside. Despite the lingering darkness of this strange day, it was Shabbat evening. She joined in the usual lighting of the Shabbat candles and group blessings, but with a heavy heart. She recalled lighting the candles each Shabbat in the weeks after her father's death—when it felt joyless and dark. Her family had felt it was important to continue this sacred devotion, but it had done little to lessen their grief. Tonight, Arava felt the importance of the ritual as well, but those dark feelings and fears persisted.

Arava had somehow held on to her belief in God. It had given her strength during the move from Galilee to Jerusalem, and eventually into the home of the high priest. Shabbat rituals and the holy day celebrations and the Scripture stories her father had taught them all sustained her. Through it all, however, she'd felt a hope for something more, something deeper. That search had been reawakened these past days as she met with Dvorah and the followers of Yeshua. Was he the Mashiach? Now he was dead.

By mustering all her energy, Arava faithfully completed her tasks that evening. With a sense of relief, she withdrew into the courtyard, but it felt cold and empty there. Even though the busy life of Caiaphas's household had returned to normal, Arava felt numb. *It's as if everything that really matters to me has been frozen in time,* she thought. *I certainly can't return to the joy I felt the day Yeshua rode into Jerusalem. But how am I going to keep going now?* With a deep sigh, she reminded herself that tomorrow might bring a better day, and after spending a few more minutes in the darkness, Arava slowly walked to her quarters to try to sleep.

11

Sudden Light

The following days were grey and lifeless for Arava. The household of Caiaphas, however, had a feeling of calm relief settle over it. The vast number of officials and leaders seeking his time had dwindled to a very few. Life had gone back to normal. Not so for Arava. She tried to go about her usual duties with as much energy as possible and to spend time alone in thought and prayer when she could. Each day she made her way to see Ezra at the gate. She felt that if Dvorah were trying to get word to her, she would likely come there. For three days, no word came.

On the third day, Ezra came early in the morning to seek her out. "Arava," he called out to her. "I know how worried you've been about the fate of your aunt. She came quietly last night and asked me to pass on this message to you. If you can get away today, she'll attempt to meet you, midmorning, at the market entrance. She emphasized that it was of extreme importance that she talk with you, so I hope you can get away." A wave of relief overcame Arava, and she thanked Ezra for looking out for her. Dvorah was still alive, and Arava had the opportunity to see her again. What had happened during the past few days since the crucifixion of Yeshua?

Arava was both excited and apprehensive about meeting with her aunt. What kinds of emotions might arise? What words of comfort could she offer? How had Dvorah reacted to the news of Yeshua's death? Was she still with his followers? Probably, seeing as she obviously hadn't left Jerusalem for home.

So many questions had been swirling around in Arava's mind. Meeting with Dvorah would hopefully bring some comfort to her, just knowing that she still had her aunt to share with. Following the morning meal, Arava secured a list of needed provisions and hurried down to the market entrance. Waiting there were Dvorah and Andrew, the disciple she had met a few days earlier. Arava took a deep breath, expecting them to be in deep sorrow. But as she drew closer, she was astounded to see that their faces were shining with joy!

"Wonderful news, Arava! It happened!" said Dvorah, pulling her niece into a secure corner.

"What happened?" she replied.

It was Andrew who gave her an answer. "Yeshua is alive! We've seen him! Yes, the crucifixion did take place, and his body was placed in a sealed tomb. But on the first day of this week, he rose from that tomb. My brother Shimon was one of the first to see the open grave and the blocking stone that had been removed. It's true—Yeshua is alive!"

Arava was totally startled. "They told me at the high priest's house that Yeshua had been crucified. No one could survive that! Caiaphas and all his household are relieved that the threat Yeshua seemed to pose has been taken care of."

Andrew continued, "Yes, Yeshua was crucified. I was not there, but Yochanan and the women sat in vigil beneath the cross. Even Yeshua's mother, Miryam, was there at the crucifixion and watched him die. It must have been horrible. But now he is alive and has appeared to many of us!"

His words were taking time to truly sink in for Arava. Yeshua was dead and buried—yet now was alive? *Does this mean that he really is the Son of God, the Anointed One, the Mashiach?*

It was Dvorah's turn to speak. "Arava, you must remember how dark it became when Yeshua was crucified. It was the darkness of dread for us. When he was arrested, we all scattered in fear. The young man John Mark tried to follow but could not. Only Shimon made it to the high priest's house."

"That must have been the person I questioned by the fire in the courtyard!" she exclaimed. "I was sure he was a disciple, but he denied ever having known Yeshua. When we confronted him, he fled."

"That indeed was my brother, Shimon," added Andrew. "He has repented in great shame for doing that. Like us, he was terrified, but he at least followed Yeshua to the high priest's when the rest of us ran away!"

Dvorah continued, "We all scattered but soon realized we needed each other at a time like this. We gathered at the home of a young follower named John Mark and his mother. The day after the crucifixion was bleak. We kept the doors locked, for we felt the authorities might hunt us down as well. After Shabbat came the wonderful news that Yeshua had risen. Now we gather in praise and wonder."

"Many of us have encountered the risen Yeshua," Andrew added, "and we're beginning to understand all that has happened. I felt the world had ended when Yeshua was crucified and buried. What's now dawning on us is that the cross was the ultimate sacrifice Yeshua made to forgive our sins. So now, as Yochanan keeps telling us, the darkness of the crucifixion day has been turned away by the brightness of God's love. That's why you found us full of joy and not sorrow today!"

This was a lot for Arava to take in. Bewildered, she wondered, *Surely it must be true. These disciples seem so confident. Dvorah certainly is convinced. But how can a dead person be raised? What will happen now?*

"Arava," continued Dvorah, "you must come and meet with us. I know it might be difficult with you living in Caiaphas's household, but if you can come and join us for our evening gathering, you may encounter Yeshua yourself. Then you will know for sure." Although Arava felt a deep, deep desire for this, she also realized the conflict it would cause with her being a servant of the high priest. She took a deep breath and thought it all over.

Deep inside, she knew that whatever the cost, she must meet with them. "I can be free to come in three days, for on that night I don't have to serve the evening meal. If you meet me at the gate, you can guide me to your meeting place." Dvorah agreed, happy to plan some more time with her niece. Soon she would return to Galilee with a few others and spread the news of Yeshua's resurrection.

So much in the past week had left Arava bewildered and troubled. She'd kept up her duties as well as she could, but anxiety and confusion had gripped her mind and her heart. Yet through it all, a slow awakening had been taking place. A rising hope had begun to grow. Encountering Yeshua and wondering if he indeed might be the Mashiach, feeling devastated when he died, dealing with the almost impossible news of the resurrection—all of that had filled Arava's mind and heart. It felt almost too good to believe! Now, though, she sensed that great possibilities lay ahead for her and her people. With the anticipation of meeting with Yeshua's followers in a few days, Arava felt a new peace.

12

Encounter

Arava suddenly awoke from a deep sleep. Rubbing her eyes, she could tell that it was still dark and that the other servants were sleeping. What had awoken her? Then she remembered the intense dream. Again, she'd been taken back to the time before her father had died so tragically. They'd been talking about his hope for an Anointed One—to deliver the people from oppression and bring about peace. Arava wondered if this dream had anything to do with her own quest to discover the true Mashiach.

Perhaps it was also because today was the day Arava would meet Dvorah and maybe even encounter the risen Yeshua! She whispered a silent message to her father. *You searched for the Mashiach. I'm so sorry for how that ended. But I have taken up your search, and now I feel I've discovered the one you were seeking. I have a new awakening in my spirit. I'm asking God to give me the wisdom to know for sure about this Yeshua. I miss you, Father, and I hope you bless me on my new journey.* That silent message brought peace to Arava, and she drifted back to sleep.

All day, she occupied herself with her daily duties, but in her heart, Arava supressed a growing excitement at what might lie ahead that night. In the darkness of evening, she waited at the gate for Dvorah. She asked Ezra to tell the night watchman that she might be coming in late. Dvorah arrived and the two of them made their way through the city. Arava suddenly remembered the disciple she'd met at the gate just before Yeshua's arrest and then again the next day. She asked Dvorah about who he might have been.

Dvorah paused for a moment and replied, "That must have been Yehuda. He bargained with the high priest, and for thirty pieces of silver, he led the crowd of soldiers and guards to arrest Yeshua. The second time you saw him would have been the day he regretted his actions and tried to return the money. Caiaphas refused him. Yehuda was rejected and dejected, and sadly, he has taken his own life. Our group of twelve disciples is now one less. Also, Tau'ma has not been joining our gatherings, although some of the disciples say they've seen him in the city."

They were now at the home where Yeshua's followers had gathered. A special knock on the door gained them entrance. However, not recognizing Arava, the woman at the door challenged her reason for being there. Dvorah assured her that Arava was a relative and was seeking to know more about the resurrection of Yeshua. There were quite a few already in the room. Arava recognized Andrew and Yaakov. Off to one side, in a deep conversation with a few others, was the man she had confronted around the fire: Andrew's brother, Shimon.

The door opened and another man entered. There was great excitement in the room, and everyone seemed eager to greet this new visitor. It didn't take Arava long to realize it must be the disciple Tau'ma, who had been missing from their gatherings.

"You may be wondering about my absence until now," he began. "I was not prepared for the arrest of Yeshua in the garden, and I fled in total panic. I hid myself in fear for many days. I had believed that, when our band arrived in Jerusalem, it would finally usher in the liberation of our nation! I watched in sorrow as Yeshua was marched off like a common criminal. I ran. I needed some time by myself to try to deal with it all. That's why I haven't been with you until now." Several of the other followers murmured, acknowledging Tau'ma's struggle. He continued, "When I received the news of his crucifixion, I was devastated. I had given everything for three years in following Yeshua, and it appeared all was lost. At least, that's how I felt at the time."

Yakov spoke up. "We do understand, Tau'ma. Most of us gathered behind these doors on that grey day after the crucifixion. We kept them locked out of fear. Would we be arrested next? We were confused and sad. But the next morning, we began to hear reports—first from these women here, then many more. The tomb was empty. Yeshua had risen and was alive. It was challenging to believe such news at first. However, later as we gathered, Yeshua appeared among us! We were amazed and filled with new hope."

"That is all good," replied Tau'ma, "but for me, I really do need to have direct proof. Unless I can put my fingers in the nail prints in his hands and the gash in his side, I can't accept Yeshua's resurrection for myself."

Arava felt a connection with this disciple. She admired his blunt honesty, for she too had struggled to comprehend the news of the resurrection of Yeshua. So many of the questions Tau'ma raised had also been on her mind. Perhaps, she thought, this gathering of disciples would provide some clear answers. Like this disciple, she felt she needed proof. A sense of gratitude arose in Arava—gratitude for this group who had welcomed her and embraced Tau'ma despite his struggles.

Suddenly a profound silence enveloped the room. All eyes turned toward a figure that had appeared in their midst. Arava was puzzled, as she had not heard anyone enter. A strange sense of quiet power and deep peace gripped them all.

"Rabbi! Master!" several voices cried out. It took Arava a few moments to realize that she was in the presence of the risen Yeshua! It was the same person she'd seen on the back of the donkey that day, but now his appearance was changed in a way Arava could not describe.

Yeshua spoke a blessing of shalom over everyone. He then made his way to stand directly in front of Tau'ma. Arava hoped Yeshua would not be too hard on him for all his questions. Contrary to that, Yeshua invited Tau'ma to touch his wounds, to experience the resurrection for himself. That was all he needed, and he knelt before Yeshua. "My Lord!" was all he said. Arava believed too. Yeshua moved through the room, speaking blessings over many.

Then, turning, he fixed his eyes on Arava. She quivered with apprehension. He spoke softly to her. "Arava, willow branch, receive the flowing Spirit of God's love. You will become a blessing far beyond this room. You will be waved before many with my peace and love." Arava took a deep breath, unable to speak. She was too moved to respond. The impact of this experience was only starting to sink in. Yeshua moved on, speaking another blessing of peace over the gathering. Then, just as mysteriously as he'd arrived, he was suddenly gone from their midst.

13

A New Beginning

Arava was still shaking from her experience. She had met the risen Yeshua! He'd spoken directly to her! Still, many thoughts and questions lingered. She was a bit perplexed over the words Yeshua had spoken. His reference to her being a willow branch felt very curious. How was she to wave God's love and peace over many? Following this encounter, others began to gather around her, touched by how Yeshua had blessed her. She asked the group about the willow branch that Yeshua had compared her to.

One of the disciples, Yochanan, spoke up. "Arava, do you remember celebrating the festival of Sukkot?" She did, for she had loved that time as a child with her family. At the gathering of the harvest, they would celebrate God's protection of the people of Israel on their journey through the wilderness and his provision for them. What she'd loved as a child was how that celebration took place. To remember the tents and shelters the Hebrew people had built in the wilderness, each family would create a sukkah, a makeshift outdoor shelter where they'd live for a week during Sukkot. Arava had thoroughly enjoyed the special family time as they constructed and then lived in their own sukkah.

Yochanan continued, "Do you recall what you would do during that time? You would take four kinds of plants: an etrog citron, a lulav palm frond, myrtle twigs, and willow branches. Remember how you waved those plants to give thanks to God. You were named after the willow branches."

Arava thought about this and said, "Yes, we waved them in six different directions." With that, she burst out, "Oh my goodness, now I remember! My parents would often tell the story of how I was born. I came rather quickly. We had been observing the festival in our sukkah, and suddenly, there I was. No chance for the midwife to be called, so my father did the delivery. My mother loved to proclaim how I took my first breath at Sukkot. Obviously, that's where my name came from. I didn't put it all together until right now!" The group all congratulated Arava as they laughed together over her story.

Yochanan concluded by affirming that, for Arava, the one named after Sukkot's willow branches, Yeshua had declared she would show God's love to the world like a waving branch. Arava had noticed this disciple who seemed to constantly glow with God's love. He counselled everyone that to truly live out the life of Yeshua, they must be prepared to love one another just as Yeshua had loved them.

Arava withdrew to a quiet corner and pondered the things that had happened to her that evening. She watched as the gathering sang praises and said prayers. She listened as they recounted more amazing stories of their time with Yeshua over the past three years. Deep feelings of peace and joy were growing inside her. After a short time, a young man came over to sit with her.

It was John Mark, whom she had briefly met before. *He's older than me but not by much*, she thought. *He certainly seems to be strongly connected to Yeshua's followers.* An infectious enthusiasm emanated from this young man. His bright shining eyes indicated a mind eager for knowledge. As he was the one individual in the group who seemed closest in age to her, Arava felt led to get to know him more.

"Shalom, Arava," he greeted her. "You have experienced so much here this evening. That was very moving, having Yeshua greet you. I hope you're not upset if I ask you a personal question. Dvorah told me that you are a servant to the high priest. Is that true?"

Arava took a moment to consider the question. She had hoped her position would not be made known, for it was Caiaphas who had demanded that Yeshua be killed. Yet she trusted this group of disciples and followers. "Yes, it is true," she replied. "I'm one of the servants who look after his household. I hope that doesn't cause you to reject me—you must realize how violently Caiaphas opposed Yeshua."

John Mark wasn't upset about her position but was more concerned about her safety if it became known she was following Yeshua. Arava had not considered that but was relieved at his concern for her. "In fact," John Mark continued, "Dvorah told me you have favour in that household and that you're often sent to secure provisions in the marketplace."

"That's the part of being a servant I enjoy most, "Arava replied. "I've become well-known to several of the shopkeepers, and I do enjoy talking with them, even bartering with them. I usually get more than I was sent for, but I can share the extra with the other servants."

"I know this is all a bit sudden for you, Arava," John Mark stated, "but I'd like you to consider joining our group. You could be a great help to us. We need to keep ourselves together until we know for certain what lies ahead. Your aunt told us of your service to Caiaphas, how you secured provisions in the market. Those contacts could really help us during this time."

Shimon joined them, obviously having overheard part of their conversation. Arava had been a bit wary of this disciple since their strange encounter around the fire in the courtyard. Shimon seemed a perplexing individual. He had the strong and calloused hands of a fisherman, just like his brother Andrew. However, he was a much larger man. More than that, Arava noticed that he seemed to dominate any conversation. You always knew when he was in the room. Andrew, on the other hand, was usually found in the background but had a knack for finding anyone who needed help. Arava wanted to talk to Shimon about that night around the fire and ask him why he had denied knowing Yeshua.

Hearing their conversation about servants, Shimon began to share his story. "Yeshua has taught me many things. It's true that in some areas, it has taken me time to really learn the truth he offered me. The night he was arrested was so powerful. Our band of disciples had met with him to celebrate Pesach. However, what really impacted me was what happened after we had settled in the upper room of John Mark's home. We were all excited and agitated. Due to that, we forgot the customary duty of one of us washing the feet of all the others. As a servant, Arava, you have probably been asked to perform that duty."

"Many times," Arava answered. "Particularly when there's a dinner to be served and many important guests arriving. To be honest, I do not always enjoy the foot washing, but it's my duty."

Shimon continued, "That night, when all of us had forgotten that duty, Yeshua himself took a bowl and towel and proceeded to wash our feet. I felt this would not do, the Mashiach himself washing our feet. I told him so, but he admonished me and said that, unless I would allow him to wash my feet, I could not be clean. I understand now that he meant spiritually clean—I needed to allow him to serve me. Yeshua then commanded me to go and wash others' feet. I realize that means a true follower must be prepared to serve others, to care for their lives and offer himself to them. Arava, in this way, being a servant for Yeshua is the greatest offering we can give."

Yochanan had quietly joined them. Like Shimon, he appeared to have been part of a small group that was close to Yeshua. "Yeshua has given us a commission to care for all his people," he began. "Arava, on your travels through the city you've surely noticed the beggars, the lame, and the infirm—and all those who have to beg to stay alive." Arava certainly had noticed them each day she ventured to the market. There were many who waited just outside the gate. Arava had always noticed them and felt a compassion for them.

She had begun to realize that due to her family situation, she, too, might have become such a beggar. Often, when she had some extra dates or figs, she would give them to one of those who waited at the entrance to the market. Particularly, she had watched for a man who'd been blind from birth. Yochanan finished by saying, "These are the people we are to serve and heal. You may have noticed that the Pharisees are very careful not to touch those people. They consider them unclean. Yeshua has directed us to go to them. Each one of them is a person created by God. No matter what their situation or story, we are to offer the compassion of Yeshua to each one."

This idea startled Arava, for she had always discounted her life as a servant girl. Now she was being challenged to see her role as having a special purpose. She had more questions for John Mark. "If I did leave the home of the high priest and join this band of followers, where would I stay?"

He replied, "We would look after you. We are doing that for others. Some of the followers living here in Jerusalem are opening their homes so our group can stay together. In fact, this upper room is part of the house where my mother and I live."

Arava did not reply—this was a lot to consider. John Mark could see her hesitation and replied, "Look, Arava, I'm not asking you to decide tonight or even right away. But please think about it and pray that God will give you direction. And I will say again, please be careful when you are at the high priest's home. We keep a watch here, for we do believe the authorities under Caiaphas may try to hunt us down. We're not afraid, however, for we know that the living Yeshua will give us protection. Now I see others getting ready to depart, so I will say goodnight to you, and I hope to see you back here very soon."

Full of thoughts and feelings, Arava suddenly realized how late it was. She made her way carefully and quickly back to Caiaphas's home, secure in knowing that the night watchman knew her and would easily allow her in. Carefully and quietly, Arava crept into the servants' quarters, as the others would already be sleeping. The past few days had felt overwhelming, and she would need some time to mull everything over. But as she lay down to sleep, Arava thought to herself, *What an experience I have had. God, where might all this be taking me? What's going to happen next?*

14

The Decision

It was the middle of the night, yet Arava could not sleep. Over the past two weeks, she'd felt like she was living two lives in two different places. The first one was right here in the home of the high priest with the other servants. That life went on day after day. In fact, she was trying to be an even better servant so as not to draw attention on the nights she left for her other life—with the followers of Yeshua. She continued to seek out provisions at the marketplace, happy to interact with shopkeepers like Mordechi and Rivkah. There was still time to explore more of the city along the way. Ezra and the night watchman at the gate had been faithful to not draw attention to the late nights when she returned.

Yet, in this life, Arava felt she had to be very careful. She remembered the caution in John Mark's voice when he'd warned her to be watchful. Caiaphas and the religious officials had conspired to kill Yeshua. Now they were aware that his followers claimed he'd risen from the dead and was still with them. Arava had heard whispers in the hallways from those officials, urging each other to watch those followers closely.

As a result, Arava was especially careful on the nights she went to the gatherings. She took different routes each time, making sure she was using some of the narrow alleyways she'd discovered during her trips to the marketplace. When she arrived at John Mark's house, where the followers were gathered, she felt a deep peace unlike any other. She listened to the stories recounted by the disciples, stories of Yeshua's three-year ministry, and her faith grew and grew. Even when Yeshua was not with them, Arava felt the embrace of his love and so often remembered the wonderful words he'd spoken to her the night she'd encountered his risen presence.

During those evening gatherings, the followers began a practice that particularly drew Arava closer to Yeshua. Shimon spoke about the Pesach seder they'd celebrated with Yeshua the night before his arrest. Arava knew the details of the seder well, and as Shimon went on, he told the group that Yeshua had done something very special during that meal. When they broke the unleavened matzah, Yeshua had told them that, from then on, this action was to represent his body, broken on the cross for their life and healing. His sacrifice was for them and for all followers in the future.

During the seder, cups of wine were blessed and shared. Shimon explained how Yeshua had taken one of the cups and changed its meaning. The cup would now represent the blood he'd shed on the cross. His blood would be a sacrifice to wash away their sins and restore a loving relationship, through him, with God. Shimon told the followers, "I've been remembering that meal and Yeshua's command to continue breaking the matzah and sharing that cup. We are to remember how he offered his life to us. Let's continue that when we gather." After Yochanan said a blessing over those two elements, everyone shared.

Arava went to John Mark's as often as she could, always taking care and caution along the way. One night, she was sure someone had tried to follow her, but she'd lost him in an alleyway. Despite the danger, she was determined to continue meeting with her new friends, for that second life was becoming far more important to her than the first. It was also causing her sleepless nights, and she knew she couldn't continue this double life for long.

The night before had been particularly powerful. As she'd arrived, John Mark had rushed up to her. "Shalom, Arava! Peace in Yeshua! Something truly amazing happened today! We had an experience that has changed us all. Come hear about it—we're about to get started." He took Arava's hand and led her to the centre of the gathering just as Shimon and Yochanan were getting up to speak.

Yochanan began, "For those of you who couldn't be with us earlier today, this is what has taken place. Yeshua told us where to meet him, and once we had all gathered, he told us that his time on earth had ended and that he would be taken back up to heaven and to God, the Father. However, he instructed us to wait here in Jerusalem for a new power, called the Holy Spirit, to come upon us."

Yochanan stood to his feet, and his voice rose with feeling as he spoke of the final moments he'd shared with his rabbi. "Yeshua then commissioned us to take his message of God's love and forgiveness out into the whole world and to share with everyone. Yeshua commanded us to go and make disciples. We are to wait for the Holy Spirit, then go out and tell everyone about God's forgiving love in Yeshua. With that he disappeared from our sight. While we are sad that he will no longer appear in our presence, we know that our lives must now be devoted to him and to reaching out with his mission. So, let's pledge ourselves to following his instructions. We'll wait here until we receive that Holy Spirit. We know that whatever happens, Yeshua will be with us."

A ripple of excitement spread across the room. John Mark turned to Arava and spoke. "You see? We have a mission! We are to be empowered by the Holy Spirit and take the love of Yeshua into all the world. We have a purpose. I'll be part of that, and you can be too. Come and join us. Take a step of faith. You won't regret it!" John Mark turned to join the gathering in singing and prayer. Taking a few moments to gather her thoughts, Arava then joined them in breaking the bread and sharing the cup— what they were now calling "communing with Yeshua."

On her way home, Arava reflected on what had been a profound evening. A deep and powerful spirit had gripped everyone in that gathering. She was aware of feeling more alive than she had ever experienced before. She knew that her awakening was coming full circle. Yet, she also realized that a decision would have to be made. Would she stay in Caiaphas's home, safe in the security it offered? Or could she take a giant step of faith and join the followers of Yeshua? She prayed for the wisdom to make the best decision.

Her moment of decision came sooner than expected. The next morning, Arava was summoned to meet with the high priest himself. The only other time she'd met with him directly was when she was first hired to work in his home. All the servants held him in great respect, a respect tinged with fear. Caiaphas was a large man who struck a very imposing presence. He constantly dressed in the long flowing robes of his station. When he spoke, it was with a loud commanding voice. Everything about this man demonstrated great power and authority.

As she made her way down the hallway to his quarters, a shiver of apprehension flowed through her. Caiaphas greeted her, then spoke directly. "Arava, you have been a faithful servant for these past three years and we value that. Unfortunately, word has come to me that you've been associating with the followers of that false Mashiach, Yeshua. You know he was crucified and buried. Surely you don't accept the nonsense going around that he's risen from the dead. We believe his followers took the body from the tomb and have hidden it."

It was all Arava could do to keep from shouting out, "You're wrong. He lives. I've met him. He has even spoken to me!"

Arava kept her silence before the high priest as he continued, "You are putting yourself in a bad position, Arava. I demand that you cease all contact with these deluded people. If you cannot, we must let you go. Remember the difficult position you were in when you started here—your father had died, and we gave you security. If you leave, you'll probably end up as a beggar around the temple. You wouldn't want that, would you? I put it to you directly, Arava. You need to set yourself straight and realize all that you have here in this household." With that, she was dismissed.

Walking slowly back to her quarters, it didn't take Arava long to make her decision. She must leave. She would take the step of faith and join with John Mark and the other followers of Yeshua. She would trust the promise that God in Yeshua would watch over her and guide her. As John Mark and Shimon had offered, she would become a new kind of servant—Yeshua's servant, living to care for his followers. She remembered the invitation she'd been given as she was leaving the night before: to join the group and celebrate the festival of Shavuot. That day was coming very soon. Arava decided that would be the day she'd arise early and leave the home of the high priest forever. She felt a deep peace. She knew that, challenging as it might be, it was the right decision!

15

Shavuot Surprise

Shavuot had arrived! Arava had packed the few possessions that meant anything to her the night before, for this time when she left the home of the high priest, she would not be returning. As the first rays of sun crept into the servants' quarters, she was already quivering with anticipation. She was about to embark on a totally new adventure. She craved the opportunity to hear more amazing stories about Yeshua, stories like the ones she'd heard so far.

During the last evening Arava had shared with the group, she'd met Miryam, the mother of Yeshua. Yochanan had advised her that Miryam would be one of those she would care for. What a privilege that will be, thought Arava, to be able to spend time with her.

Still, Arava had felt somewhat apprehensive before her first meeting with Miryam. She was, after all, the Lord's mother. Arava wondered about all the experiences Mirriam would have had during her life with Yeshua. Were the stories about the birth in Bethlehem true? How had Miryam been able to stand at the foot of the cross and watch her son suffering?

Miryam had been delighted when she first met Arava and learned that she'd grown up in Cana. "I have been there many times," said Miryam. "Do you know that my Yeshua performed a miracle in Cana?" Arava had not heard about this miracle. Perhaps it had occurred after she'd left for Jerusalem.

"We were together at a wedding feast in Cana," Miryam had continued. "It was going well, but the host ran out of wine. Yeshua commanded huge jars of water to be turned into wine. And do you know what, Arava?" Arava had been mystified. Miryam clapped her hands and declared, "That water became the best-tasting wine ever! You should have been there!" They'd had a good chuckle over that. Now Arava felt even more at home with these loving friends and was ready for her role in serving.

Yochanan had spoken further with Arava about the importance of being Yeshua's servant. "We are to love one another," he'd outlined. "That is the essential truth I learned from Yeshua. We are called to care for all people, particularly those who need love the most. Yeshua taught that, when he was no longer with us, we would discover him by showing love to those in need. When you feed the hungry, clothe the naked, or give a drink to a thirsty person, you are offering that love to Yeshua himself." Arava was beginning to realize what her purpose would be for the rest of her life: serving Yeshua!

Today they would celebrate Shavuot, and Arava recalled that time from her childhood. Fifty days following Pesach, Shavuot was a celebration of the first harvest of the year. Arava fondly recalled her experience as a child joining the village's celebration of the harvest, giving thanks to God for his bounty and blessing. As she rose that morning, Arava took a few minutes in thankful praise for all that had happened in her life leading to this day.

Arava particularly loved Shavuot for the Scripture story that was retold every year. It was the story of Reut and Naomi. Naomi, her husband, and two sons had to leave Israel due to a severe drought and settle in Moab, a foreign land. The two sons married Moabite women, but both those sons and Naomi's husband died. When Naomi knew it was safe to return home to Israel, only one daughter-in-law, Reut, chose to go with her, pledging to stay with her forever. To survive in Israel, Reut had to glean grain from the harvest fields. The owner, Boaz, made sure there was grain left for the gleaners. The story ended with Reut and Boaz meeting and marrying. Arava loved that story, for it captured her imagination and caused her to wonder if someday God might put her in a position to fall in love like he had Reut. Arava felt a truth settle in her heart. *God indeed can bless us with dreams for the future. I pray that God has a plan for me and will guide me as I go forward!*

However, she must first deal with her present reality. Today she would begin a new life with the followers of the risen Yeshua. Arava took one last look behind her, saying a thank you to Ezra as he let her out through the gate. She had confided to him that she wouldn't see him again, trusting him not to divulge anything to Caiaphas. The evening before, she'd been able to talk with Hadassah and thank her for all the support she'd provided. They had parted tearfully.

It took her longer than usual to reach the home where the followers were gathered. Once again, she sensed she was being followed. Perhaps Caiaphas had guessed what her decision would be after demanding she remain with his household. Arava took a rambling route through the city, down different streets and alleyways, until she was sure that whoever was following her had disappeared. She arrived later than she'd anticipated.

She was surprised when she reached John Mark's house. The followers of Yeshua had spilled out into the surrounding streets. Loud shouts of praise reached her ears. Even more, many of the followers were speaking in languages Arava did not understand. This was attracting many people. Some of them were exclaiming how news of Yeshua was being proclaimed in their own native languages. This was amazing!

Finally, Arava found John Mark and exclaimed, "What in the world is going on? I was expecting a celebration of the feast of Shavuot, but what is all this?"

With great excitement, John Mark replied, "Just as Yeshua promised, the Holy Spirit has arrived! You should have been here earlier, for it felt like a mighty, rushing wind, and it seemed like tongues of fire hovered over us. We all feel a power unlike anything we've sensed before. Can you feel it too, Arava?"

Arava had to admit she felt an energy surging inside her. "Is this the power that will enable us to live out Yeshua's love to the whole world?"

John Mark didn't have time to answer, for Shimon began to speak in a bold, loud voice. He assured the curious onlookers that, although it might appear Yeshua's followers were drunk, that was certainly not the case. He explained that this was a fulfillment of the proclamation from the prophet Joel—that at the appointed time, God would pour out his Spirit. Today was the day it was taking place. Shimon then presented the story of Yeshua, how he was crucified but rose again. He invited everyone to become followers, to accept Yeshua as Saviour and Lord, just as Arava had done.

Arava stood amazed and perplexed. Was this not the fearful man from a few weeks before who had flatly denied even knowing Yeshua as they sat around the fire? She'd heard that Shimon had been a fisherman along with some of the other disciples.

He did appear a bit rough at times. He could go from fearful to bold in an instant. Arava realized that she was somewhat like that too. Her life over the past week had been filled with a dramatic mix of hope and apprehension. Despite that, a new boldness had been awakened in her. She had been able to take the risk of leaving Caiaphas's household, and here she was, willing to embark on a whole new life!

Drawn back to what was happening around her, Arava saw that a great mass of people had responded to Shimon's speech. Despite the authorities' confidence that they had eliminated Yeshua, the movement was suddenly growing in strength and numbers. Arava was exhilarated. She was now part of this wonderful group of believers. After all her struggles, she felt she'd finally, truly arrived at where God wanted her to be. Later that night, she mulled over the amazing day. She was lodged with close friends of John Mark and his mother, along with two other followers of Yeshua. Where might God be taking her?

16

Forgiveness

Following Shavuot, time seemed to speed up for Arava. She applied herself to her new serving role, and there certainly was a great need. Miracles were happening, such as the time Yochanan reported a crippled man being cured at the temple. Arava could just imagine this man suddenly walking and leaping and praising God! The gatherings were powerful, filled with singing and prayer and the communion they shared.

Arava found her time with Yeshua's followers and disciples to be truly life changing. Disciples like Shimon and Yaakov shared many stories of the three years they'd spent with their rabbi in Galilee. Arava recognized the names of many of the places there, such as Capernaum and Magdala. She was also spending a lot of time with John Mark. Not having been with Yeshua during those years in Galilee, he seemed particularly focused on learning as much as he could about the disciples' experiences.

"I believe it will be of vital importance for us to preserve all these stories," he told Arava, "so we can share them with those who come after us—those who never had the opportunity to meet Yeshua. That's why this time is so important. We can be with those who shared in the Lord's ministry. You've heard some of their wonderful accounts. Shimon particularly recounts some amazing stories about his time as a disciple. We must find a way to preserve them."

Immediately, John Mark and Arava recalled a dramatic story Shimon had shared the night before. He'd told them about the time Yeshua had taken three disciples, including Shimon, up on a mountain to pray. As they were praying, they'd suddenly noticed that Yeshua was being changed before their eyes. His appearance had been dazzling. Even more than that, Moses and Elijah had appeared to converse with him. The whole experience had been overpowering for Shimon, and he'd asked Yeshua to stay on that mountain and extend their time there. The Lord had not agreed. They'd descended the mountain only to encounter a situation with a man who'd brought his son for healing. Shimon had shrugged, saying it was a riveting experience on the mountain, but reality was always there waiting, demanding more time from Yeshua to love and heal broken people.

Stories like this one only reinforced what John Mark was saying about preserving the accounts of Yeshua's ministry. Arava had begun to treasure these accounts, and she realized how important hearing from the disciples had become for her—and how much more she desired to learn. "Perhaps you could help me with that," continued John Mark. "You certainly have a bright, inquisitive mind, and we could share the stories we hear with each other to ensure we remember them correctly." Arava eagerly agreed to assist John Mark in any way she could, excited about the possibility of hearing more about Yeshua's ministry.

Arava wanted to ask Shimon personally about that night around the courtyard fire. She needed a resolution to such a strange encounter. A few days later, she spotted him sitting quietly, enjoying the dates she'd secured at the market. She approached and greeted him by asking if he was enjoying the food. "Oh, thank you so much, Arava," he replied. "These dates are so fresh! How are you getting along here with our group of followers?" She told him she was happily surprised at how warmly she'd been accepted into the group, and by how much she was learning and growing. Indeed, she was truly experiencing more of Yeshua's love every day.

Then she asked Shimon directly, "Do you remember the night of Yeshua's arrest?"

"It is still vivid in my mind," replied Shimon. "Sharing the Pesach seder and listening to the words of Yeshua that night was profound. We went to the olive grove called Gethsemane, down in the Kidron Valley at the foot of the Mount of Olives. Yeshua took a few of us aside, as he desired to pray. Sadly, we fell asleep—not once but numerous times. We were all startled when Yehuda simply walked up to Yeshua, kissed him, and identified him as the one to be arrested. We panicked and scattered. I had promised Yeshua that I would stick by him, and so I followed the guards to the high priest's."

"I know that," responded Arava. "I was there in the courtyard when they brought Yeshua to be questioned by Annas and Caiaphas."

Shimon's eyes widened. "Then that was you who first challenged me by the fire!"

"Yes," Arava answered. "I was so confused by the way you denied ever knowing Yeshua."

"I was frozen in terror," Shimon said, "and just blurted it out. I soon realized what I'd said and fled in shame. I felt that I'd let down everything I had lived for with Yeshua for the past three years. My courage evaporated, and I was overwhelmed with fear. I was such a failure in not standing up to defend him. I felt like I was responsible for allowing him to be crucified."

He continued, "I had a hard time getting over that, but I knew my life was with the other disciples and followers, and so I returned to this upper room where they had regrouped. Thankfully, they accepted me—for they had scattered on the night of the arrest as well. Of course, everything changed when we realized Yeshua had risen from that tomb. I want to add something that's become very important to me. One day, a few of us went back to Galilee and decided to try fishing again. A lot happened that day. Yeshua met us. He took me aside and asked me three times if I still loved him. I replied that I did, and he commissioned me to feed his sheep! I knew that I was totally forgiven for my denial. I was freed to serve Yeshua just as I am now doing."

Arava was taking in all that Shimon was sharing with her. "I'm beginning to grasp the essence of Yeshua's forgiveness myself," she said. "Perhaps Yeshua would have forgiven my father for following a false Mashiach, getting killed, and leaving our family devastated."

Shimon paused and replied, "I am sure that he would, Arava. He would acknowledge your father's desire to see the fulfillment of an Anointed One. Just look at how Yeshua has entered your life to fulfill your father's dreams."

"There's something else, Shimon," Arava continued. "Some intense and disturbing feelings have been awakened in me since I've come to fully comprehend my father's death. The most difficult is a deep feeling of anger toward him—anger that he took that risk, got killed, and abandoned our family. I also have deep resentment against the Roman soldiers who killed my father and the others that day. It's created a great fear of anything to do with Rome."

Yochanan had quietly come to sit down beside Shimon and Arava. He spoke up. "You know, Arava, how much I talk about Yeshua's love—how we are to love him and love one another. Think about this: Yeshua understands exactly what you've been feeling and does not judge you for feeling guilty about those angry emotions. You cared so much for your father, and you always will. Remember, you cannot undo the past actions that he took. Know that God is extending his love and strength to you."

Speaking softly now, Yochanan added, "Arava, hold on to the stronger sense that you are fulfilling your father's dreams. Particularly right now, when you are living out the love of God in Yeshua by serving others. God has brought much good out of the difficult circumstances of your past. Pray for forgiveness for those Roman soldiers. Yeshua told us to pray for our enemies, to love them. I truly believe that the message of Yeshua will soon be offered to the Romans. You are free now to serve Yeshua. Perhaps you will have a part in his mission into all the world! Remember the words Yeshua said to you that night. You are to be like a willow branch of love waved before the world. I am sure you will have a wonderful future!" With that, the conversation ended. Arava truly felt blessed by those two faithful disciples.

A peace descended upon the room. Arava reflected on all they had shared with her. She turned to Shimon, thanking him for his honesty about the night around the fire in the courtyard. "You see how far we've come since then, Arava. What seemed at first like the end of all things for us, was actually just the beginning. Who knows where Yeshua will lead us?"

Epilogue

To the Ends of the Earth

Arava's new life in the company of Yeshua's followers was exhilarating. There were, however, growing tensions as well. She knew only too well that the high priest would hear of the movement and do everything to stop it. Shimon and Yochanan were commanded to appear before the council, but they continued to be bold in their faith. Sadly, a wonderful man Arava had just come to know, Stephen, was arrested and stoned to death. The followers deeply grieved this loss, but it emboldened them even more. Yeshua had warned them about persecution. Some in the group left Jerusalem to seek safety elsewhere. Dvorah was preparing to return to Galilee as well.

Many of the followers shared what they had for the common good. Arava and John Mark used some of this money to purchase food and provisions in the market. The number of people joining Yeshua's followers meant increasing needs. Arava discovered a special role in supporting a growing number of widows. From her earlier experience, she knew just how difficult life could be for a woman whose husband had died. That had certainly been the case for her mother. It had been quite a revelation for Arava to discover that God could transform her painful past into a special compassion for others.

New followers were arriving from many different places. One man Arava came to know well was Yosef, who had come from the island of Cyprus. He was a kind, thoughtful, and loving man. Arava enjoyed the long talks they had together. These were times when she could share her heart with someone who listened carefully and encouraged her. Others in the group felt the same. They gave Yosef the name "Barnabas," which meant "son of encouragement." Arava felt the name fit him well and was glad to have him to confide in.

Barnabas shared the story of how he'd come to Jerusalem. Arava listened with great interest as he described living on the island of Cyprus in the Mediterranean Sea. She could hardly comprehend such a vast body of water and thought that one day she must see it for herself. Barnabas had grown up in a Jewish home but had responded to the good news of Yeshua. He'd become convinced that Yeshua was the true Mashiach. Out of that experience, he'd made the decision to journey to Jerusalem and join with Yeshua's followers.

"You see," he said to her with a smile, "you and I have some similar experiences. We both came from small places, took a risk, and made the journey to this large and dramatic city. Both of us have discovered Yeshua and found a new home with his followers. God has given each of us a special role to serve him and live out the love and compassion of Yeshua!" Clapping his hands, he exclaimed, "Isn't it a miracle?"

There was talk of a religious official named Saul, a leading member of the Pharisees who'd led the persecution of Yeshua's followers. By now, they'd begun to refer to themselves as followers of the Way. Yochanan reminded them that Yeshua had called himself the way, the truth, and the life. News came that Saul had had an encounter with Yeshua and was turning to embrace the faith. He now wanted to be part of the Way as it expanded. Barnabas spoke quite a bit about this with Arava and John Mark, as he felt it could help move the faith forward. But because of Saul's history of persecuting Yeshua's followers, others in the group were skeptical.

The day arrived for Dvorah to return to Galilee. Before her departure, she drew Arava aside to share her plans. "I'll be returning to Capernaum, which is my home now and was also the centre for Yeshua's ministry in Galilee," she began. "There are followers there who need to know everything about the crucifixion and resurrection. A few of us are going, and we plan to share about the coming of the Holy Spirit and our ministry to tell the news of Yeshua far and wide."

"Will you go back to Cana?" asked Arava.

"Oh yes, for I do miss all our family there. I'll seek out your mother, Arava, and let her know that you are well. May I share about you joining our band of followers?"

"Please do," replied Arava. "I wonder what my mother will think about everything that's happened to me."

"I know your mother well," Dvorah added, "and I imagine she will say you are so much like your father!"

"I think so as well," Arava replied. "I realize now that my father nurtured my curiosity, especially about God and the Scriptures. I've also realized that I got my zeal to care for others from my mother. She did so much for all of us. I do pray that she's well. If you have an opportunity, please tell my brother and sister how much I miss them and love them. I pray for them every day."

Dvorah promised Arava that, if possible, she would send word to her about her mother. Arava would miss her times with Dvorah but realized that her future now lay in following the risen Yeshua. She said a blessing over Dvorah and bid her goodbye.

God had plans for Arava as well. A short time later, Barnabas took her and John Mark aside and described a growing gathering of followers in a city called Antioch. Arava had never heard of that place. It seemed to be a long distance away in a foreign land. However, Barnabas was going there to support the new followers.

"Antioch is a large, important city," he said to Arava. "It's amazing how quickly news of Yeshua has caught on there. I hear that many have joined the followers of the Way who journeyed there to proclaim our faith. In fact, many of the new believers are from all backgrounds. The group here in Jerusalem wants me to go and encourage them."

Then Barnabas looked straight at her and said, "I will be leaving in a week, Arava, and I want you to come with me. I realize it will involve a long journey and an adjustment to a very different city. However, I believe you could be of great help in Antioch. I've asked John Mark as well, and he will be coming to Antioch shortly. What do you think?"

Arava was startled by this invitation. Her life had come a long way from her childhood in Cana. She'd been totally changed by encountering Yeshua in Jerusalem. Her life as a servant to the high priest had been transformed into serving the risen Yeshua. She had settled into her life with his followers, feeling accepted and loved. She had developed special relationships with many of the disciples and with Miryam. It would be hard to leave all that now.

Arava also realized that the situation was changing. Many were moving out into places like this city, Antioch. Now a new challenge had been presented to her by Barnabas. Perhaps it was the Holy Spirit, but almost without thinking, Arava agreed to go. She would be bold, knowing Yeshua would be with her. She could not imagine what lay ahead, but it was reassuring that

Barnabas would be with her. She was very pleased to hear that John Mark would be coming too.

Later that day she sought out John Mark. "Barnabas has asked me to travel with him to Antioch, and I believe he's approached you as well," she began. "What do you think about that idea?"

John Mark replied, "Arava, let me begin by saying how happy I've been that you accepted my challenge and joined us here. I felt from the beginning that you would be a valued servant of Yeshua, and that has proven true. But, more than that, I've appreciated the time we spend together. It has been wonderful to be able to share our thoughts and questions. I treasure the times we've sat and listened to the disciples tell their stories. I believe we now have a solid collection of the most powerful accounts of Yeshua."

He continued, "We both know things have changed here with the increased pressure from the religious authorities. I believe that also gives us a new opportunity to take the message of Yeshua far beyond Jerusalem. Initially, when I spoke with Barnabas, I didn't want to accept the offer to travel to Antioch. It seemed so far away, and I wasn't sure I would be up to the work he felt I could accomplish there. But you know Barnabas. He kept encouraging me to accept. I believe he's looking at a ministry that goes beyond Antioch into the Roman world—and he wants us to be a part of that. With that, I agreed, and I hope you have too!"

Arava replied, "Much of what you are telling me is what I have been feeling as well. When I made the decision to join you and the followers of Yeshua here, I realized the big step I was taking. Working for Caiaphas did give me security. But I'm so glad I accepted your challenge and joined. I sense going to Antioch will be similar. In the time I've spent here, I have felt safe and secure. The love of all the followers, the message of Yeshua, and the power of the Holy Sprit have enabled me to grow. I realize now that what I've received, I need to offer to others, whether in Antioch or beyond. So, John Mark, let's take another great step in the name of Yeshua!"

The next morning, Arava awoke with excitement. She had to admit, however, that she still felt a degree of apprehension over this sudden development in her life. She took some time that morning to wander the streets and passageways of Jerusalem that had become familiar to her over the past three years. Her footsteps took her to the foot of the Temple Mount where she gazed up once more at the magnificent edifice gleaming in the morning sun. She would miss this amazing city with all its history and intrigue. She'd hold tightly to the memories of the dramatic time she had lived through.

Despite that, Arava was filled with tremendous excitement about moving on. *I wonder what Antioch will be like*, she pondered. Jerusalem was so much different than Cana, and now Antioch would be another adventure, a new place to explore and experience. She hoped they would have a great market there. *It will be interesting to meet the shopkeepers in that place*, she thought. Thankfully, Arava remembered, she would be with fellow followers of Yeshua. She would travel with Barnabas. Soon, John Mark would come. Arava determined to make a new home for herself in Antioch. She would be serving Yeshua with love and compassion for everyone she met.

That evening, she set to gathering her few possessions once again. A new chapter in her life was unfolding. Perhaps she would experience even more awakenings in her spirit. Once again, she felt a great peace. She had made the right decision! Arava's heart stirred with faith as she prepared to walk toward God's adventure for her in Antioch.

Afterword

You have joined Arava on her awakening journey to discover Jesus. Was Arava a real person? This novel is based on one reference in the Bible, the reference to a servant girl who confronted Simon Peter on the night of Jesus' arrest. You can find that reference in Matthew 26:69, Mark 14:66–67, and Luke 22:56. Using that reference, I gave the servant girl a name: Arava. I built a story of what her life might have been like before that episode with Simon Peter and what might have happened to her in the days and months following. I felt that, after this simple encounter, Arava's entire life was changed.

Arava's quest to discover the true Messiah led to the awakening of many thoughts and feelings within her, leading her to accept Jesus and join his early disciples and followers after the resurrection. Perhaps your heart has been awakened as well to the reality of Jesus—God's Son and Messiah. I invite you to seek out the followers of Jesus in the world today. Look for a church or small group in which you feel welcome, a group that is willing to answer any questions you may have and encourage your spirit's awakening to Jesus' loving presence.

As author of this novel, I am approachable as well and would be happy to hear from you through email: tedcreen@hotmail.com.

I pray that this novel has been both exciting and thought-provoking for you and that your connection with Jesus has deepened.

www.ingramcontent.com/pod-product-compliance
Lightning Source LLC
Chambersburg PA
CBHW030237180626
46810CB00008B/3174